Martin Combe, Duncan Lisle

**Arnold Robur**

A Novel: Vol.III.

Martin Combe, Duncan Lisle

**Arnold Robur**
*A Novel: Vol.III.*

ISBN/EAN: 9783337067762

Printed in Europe, USA, Canada, Australia, Japan

Cover: Foto ©Andreas Hilbeck / pixelio.de

More available books at **www.hansebooks.com**

# ARNOLD ROBUR.

## VOL. III.

# A Novel

## By MARTIN COMBE

### AND

## DUNCAN LISLE

*IN THREE VOLUMES*

VOL. III.

.

LONDON: CHAPMAN AND HALL

Limited

1886

# CONTENTS OF VOLUME III.

## CHAPTER I.

PAGE

WISDOM OR FOLLY?  ...  ...  ...  ...  1

## CHAPTER II.

CROSS QUESTIONS AND CROOKED ANSWERS  ...  ...  22

## CHAPTER III.

SQUIRES AND DAMES  ...  ...  ...  ...  49

## CHAPTER IV.

" A GENTLEMAN TO SEE YOU"  ...  ...  ...  74

## CHAPTER V.

" HONOUR THY FATHER"  ...  ...  ...  97

## CHAPTER VI.

GIBBINS TAKES OFF HIS COAT  ...  ...  ...  124

## CHAPTER VII.

GUESSED WRONG  ...  ...  ...  ...  139

## CHAPTER VIII.

PAGE

UNRESPITED ... ... ... ... ... 161

## CHAPTER IX.

CONTRA MUNDUM ... ... ... ... 177

## CHAPTER X.

PENITENTS ... ... ... ... ... 200

## CHAPTER XI.

OUTSIDE THE STATION ... ... ... ... 222

## CHAPTER XII.

INSIDE THE STATION ... ... ... ... 251

## CHAPTER XIII.

WHOLESALE BUSINESS ... ... ... ... 261

## CHAPTER XIV.

JOANNA LOOKS OUT OF THE WINDOW ... ... 285

# ARNOLD ROBUR.

## CHAPTER I.

### WISDOM OR FOLLY?

"The noble mansion is most distinguished by the beautiful
images it retains of beings passed away; and so is the
noble mind."—*Landor.*

ARNOLD's sudden return was a surprise to the
simple priest and priestess of his household gods.
To Barbara it came at first as a pleasurable
shock. But bodily presence is a poor compensation for absence of mind. The sympathetic
creature felt that her enquiries and her company
were alike irksome to her master, and soon
descended to her room down-stairs with so woe-
begone an expression on her fallen countenance
that Gibbins, who was waiting there to hear
what news she brought, grew instantaneously
hopeful. In a moment the depression which
normally affected his mental atmosphere had
cleared away. For the nonce his star was in

the ascendant, and seemed to twinkle as brightly as could be desired.

"Bin a knockin' of his 'ead up agin a brick wall this time, eh, mum?"

There was a subdued ring of conviction about the remark that made it sound less like a question than an assertion.

"I wish you'd try it on yourself, Joshua Gibbins," retorted the housekeeper, quite viciously for her. "Only don't do it here," she added with bitter sarcasm; "I can't have the place littered up with sawdust and bran; Rhoda's got enough to do without any extra sweeping."

Here was a thunder-clap! Could any sane bailiff—and to be a bailiff a man must be very sane indeed—have believed it possible that she, Barbara Marchpane, the mildest, most equable of matrons, should so far forget herself as to indulge in speculations of a personal nature relative to the contents of his cranium? If there had been any provocation, now, the case would have been different.

"Their tempers is awful screwy," mused Joshua, veiling under the discreet generality of the plural an express allusion to one member of the sex to which this somewhat elliptical proposition was doubtless intended to refer.

"Not all the orange-peel," he went on sententiously, addressing the offender aloud, "not

all the orange-peel of all the oranges what
growed on all the orange-trees since the world
began, Mrs. Marchpane, mum, hev caused so
many slips as reddycule."

"Stuff and nonsense! you and your orange-
peel! I've no patience with you, Joshua."
She could not help smiling a little, however, and
a smile chases the wrinkles from one's brow, do
what one will.

"Very well, mum, as you please. But, all
the same, what I maintains is that for general
slippyness, and being a orkard thing to handle,
so to speak, reddycule and greasy poles ain't
to be named together." With these words Mr.
Gibbins rose and retired with ponderous sedateness, leaving the lady to think better of it.

"There ain't no 'int of nothink Pharisee-like
about me," reflected he as he wended his way
towards the farmyard, "and as for being stuck-
uppish, I can take my oath as there ain't a
ewe-lamb what knows its place more'n what I
do. But if there is anythink as I can't stum-
mick it is for her to take and use me for a
laughin'-stick. Not as I likes any one to do it;
but it's wuss when she breaks out a reddyculin',
'cos she knows how it's got to be done in a way
that's jest downright sinful." He stooped to
fasten one of his gaiters which was flapping.
"Some day I shall up'n answer her, I specks,

when she's in one o' these 'ere reddyculin'
humours.  P'raps she don't know how near she
was gettin' blistered arter what she said just
now.  But there, what do I care for her in-you-
enters?   'Tain't as if I didn't know what's
inside o' here," and he tapped his head.  " Only
let her mind she don't go too fur, and drive me
past where I won't stand no more badgerin';
that's all."

Joshua was as near an actual ebullition of
spleen that afternoon as it was possible for him
to be.  He was annoyed that Arnold did not
send for him to consult about matters on the
estate.  But the evening wore away without
any sign on the part of the master that he
wished to be disturbed from his privacy; and
Gibbins had to content himself with a game of
cribbage, over which he squared his little difference with Barbara by having all the luck on his
side, and beating her to fits—of laughter.  After
this he became much more charitable towards
her, explaining her mistakes with compassionate
superiority, and thereby successfully propitiating
her till she grew communicative once more, and
allowed him to extract from her the little she
knew about Arnold's condition.

Meanwhile our hero was having a restless time
enough.  His mood was not an amiable one,
nor did it console him to remember that, after

all, he had no right to be angry: If Ursula
chose to like someone else better, what could it
matter to him who that someone might happen
to be ? His thoughts harped upon the early
days of his suspense, before the agitation which
it occasioned had grown so acutely painful as it
had been of late. The memory of that time
rose up vividly before him now. Uncertainty
had grown and grown till it became his bug-
bear. "Let me be sure of what is to be," he
had cried, "and this cup of agony shall pass
from me."

Well, he was sure now, and things seemed
worse than ever. Would they remain so ?
There was no longer any one to please but himself, and life was straightway become no longer
desirable. Irony of circumstances ! He had
caught a glimpse of enjoyment so high and pure
that it had dazzled him, and threatened to make
him blind to every other delight in the future.
Having once tasted nectar and ambrosia, how
was it possible to put up with beef and beer for
the rest of his existence ?

He took up the lamp with a sigh, and began
to scan the book-shelves for a likely adviser.
Some old classic was the thing he wanted, something to stimulate him with its crisp Pagan
freshness, something which required concentra-
tion, too, for all its simplicity, that his thoughts

might have · less chance of recurring to their unblest monotony of retrospection.

It was some time before he found it, and dragged it eagerly from its retreat.

"*Theocritus!* The very fellow! Come, my friend; you shall sing me to sleep."

He threw himself into his chair, trimmed the lamp, and opened the vellum-bound volume. It was the copy in which he had first become acquainted with the treasures of the old Sicilian poet, and he had never known another. The influence of old associations was upon him, and he was speedily absorbed in a sweet pastoral melody. The goatherd's passionate outcries, his hopes and fears, his diffidence and his assurance, his morbid sensitiveness to any trifle which might have the least imaginary connexion with the fair nymph who shut out from him all else that the universe contained of beauty,—all this was so true a type of what they feel who are possessed by the divine frenzy of love that the bitterness of baulked ambition in Arnold must have been doubly intensified, and a new poignancy added to it, but for the unutterable spell of those potent numbers which allay with their subtle thrill of bliss the throbbing of awakened grief. The general effect of the idyll upon the reader was inexplicably sedative. He turned over the leaves dreamily till they lay open at the page where the rude Cyclops shows himself transformed into a tractable and amiable monster by a mermaid's unkind witchery. There was a fascination that could not be resisted in this picture of the metamorphosed Polyphemus, a truculent cannibal changed into a gentle and venerable hermit. No portent this, but an ageless truism; no illusion depending upon that graceful legerdemain which has passed away with the spirit of antique song; but a reality still, in spite of the narrow exactitude of bloated science, and the rancorous babble of specialists. A clown has as much chance of becoming a gentleman to-day as his "rude forefather" had two thousand years ago. The grace of chivalry, the refinement of saintliness, seek shelter everywhere and everywhen, and decorate their tenements with a glory not widely different from that which once hallowed a stable for Love's mighty advent.

But the poor heathen Cyclops knew nothing of this, and consequently there is a sordid touch about the conclusion of his lament which grates upon the modern reader with its too practical consideration of ways and means for the attainment of something to stay the pang of baffled passion. It may be very pleasant and comfortable for the lover to be able to console himself with the inspiring reflection that a bird in the

hand is worth two in the bush, or that there are
more and better Galateas in the sea than ever
came out of it, but he ceases to interest farther
after the expression of such opinions. A con-
temptuous "God-speed, good Cyclops!" and
that cautious hero is forgotten. There is no
such phrase as *second best* in the vocabulary of
love. *One thing or nothing* is the legend on its
standards, which accounts quite as much for its
many victories as for its numerous defeats.

Arnold had had his fill of Theocritus. He
closed the book, feeling restored by its sweetness, but not inclined to be amused by its
cynicism. He was more than ever conscious
that no one was to blame for his misery. He had
got the certainty which he had demanded; that
was all. An ugly shock it was, to be sure, but
ought he not to rejoice that it had not been
deferred till it would have been even harder to
bear? He would do nothing hastily or wildly;
no wretched impulse of pique or animosity
should sway him. Not that he could ever
forget her,—at least, so it seemed to him now,—
nor did he intend to try. Time would sweeten
and purify her memory for him, but could not
obliterate it. Why should the thought of her
cease to animate him, now that he was deprived
merely of that close union which he had panted
for? An idealised conception of her was still

possible,—might be more possible, when once
the grief of seeming separation was assuaged,
and there could be no danger of her falling short
of his idea. It was somewhat early to form
these new hopes, and he came very near breaking down in the attempt. But by little and
little he grew calmer than he had been for long,
and was able to see how much good might yet
be extracted from life. If sympathy and, in
some sense, companionship are essential to
happiness, these blessings may be enjoyed without actual engagements or marriages, and it does
not necessarily follow that such institutions are
always sure of achieving the end for which they
are designed. Circumstances may unfortunately
occur to make enforced and insoluble unions the
reverse of companionable or sympathetic. Not
that anything would be gained by dwelling on
such chances before there is any probability of
their coming to pass. Wiseacres might have
consoled themselves by saying that Arnold and
Ursula were too much alike to suit each other;
for Arnold it was enough to know that, had he
been worthy of everything else in the world
twice over, he could never have deserved his
lady's regard.

Next morning he was up betimes, and, in the
determination not to be crushed or dejected, sent
for Gibbins immediately after breakfast.

"Glad to see you a-lookin' so well, sir," was that functionary's first remark on entering the room; "maybe you'll stop and cheer us up a bit now you're back among us agin. We've bin powerful lonesome and down-sperited since you left us, Mr. Arnold."

"Why, how's that, Gibbins? What's become of the 'brighter side'?"

"Well, sir, it's bin a-keepin' wonderful dark lately, to be sure; but I s'pose it's there all the same."

"Gibbins," said Arnold encouragingly, "you are the apocalypse of common-sense!"

"Ah," ejaculated the bailiff, drawing a long breath, and stepping back suddenly as if he were rather overpowered by the compliment; "there's more in that 'ere name than meets the hear, Mr. Arnold, as you and I knows, sir. Now a outsider might hev said it was aboose. I've half a mind to try it on Mrs. Marchpane, and see how she takes it."

A harmless threat, for he had completely forgotten the phrase, if he had ever caught it; but it alarmed Arnold.

"No, don't do that," he said hastily; "it was only my fun, you know, and she wouldn't understand it as you do."

"Very well, sir," replied Gibbins with dignity; "I think it 'ud please her; but, hows'ever, your bein' so set agin it putts the whole matter on a private and confident footin', and I ain't a-goin' to whisper none o' your secrets, sir; rest upon me."

Arnold's mind was relieved. He unlocked a drawer, and produced some folded sheets of foolscap. Handing them to his companion he requested him to tell him if he had ever seen them before. Gibbins fumbled in his pocket, and produced an enormous pair of spectacles of extremely massive workmanship. Carefully adjusting this engine,—for no other word can aptly describe so ponderous a structure,—he brought the document into focus with elaborate precision, and delivered himself of the laconic rejoinder, " Ezactly."

" You recognize those papers ? "

But Joshua Gibbins was not the man to transact business with unseemly haste, and it was not until he had gingerly removed the spectacles from his nose, and ceremoniously restored them to his voluminous coat-tail, as though he were afraid of the disastrous effect upon them of such unusual wear and tear, that he replied :

" In course I minds 'em, sir. Why, I see that 'ere inwention drawed up by the clerk what was sent down to do it after your poor mother died, Mr. Arnold, and you was left a hinfant-at-arms, as the lawyers say. And I won't deny as I had

a 'and in it myself, sir," he added, a pardonable
pride suffusing his sagacious visage, as he gave
the papers back to their owner.

Joshua's phraseology was wont to be a trifle
mixed, and the distinction between an invention
and an inventory seems to have been scarcely less
obscure to him than that nautical problem con-
cerning rudder and bowsprit which is related to
have puzzled certain voyagers of classic renown.

" Somebody has put a foot as well as a hand in
it, I should say," observed Arnold ; " anyhow, it's
full of mistakes.    There are things down in it
that I can't find, and some things aren't mentioned at all."

" Now that's a rum go, that is."    Gibbins
scratched his head comprehensively.

" I'll be sworn everythink as I know'd on was
put down in they bits o' paper," he went on ;
" seems like as if they must a' got rubbed out
arterwards.    No, sir ; a rummier go never went,
sure-ly."

Arnold's sole object in thus cross-questioning
his faithful retainer was to get at the truth about
his mother's ring, which was included in the
inventory of her jewels, but was not to be found
among them.    But, eager as he was to satisfy his
natural curiosity upon this point, he did not want
to be the first to mention the missing heirloom,
being fearful of hurting the feelings of the honest

bailiff. Besides, he had known of the loss for some time without making any enquiries about it, and he could not explain to Gibbins the fresh impetus which he had received from recent events to investigate the matter. He therefore persevered in his circuitous method of examination, hoping that the examinee might presently throw some accidental light on the mystery of his own accord.

"Take the pictures, for instance," resumed Arnold. "Here's one in the inventory described as 'portrait of a gentleman'; but I've never been able to discover it."

"That's all right, sir," responded Gibbins cheerfully; "there's the article in question," and he jerked his thumb at a painting which was hanging on the wall behind his chair.

"Why, but that's a picture of St. Peter, by Correggio; I was just coming to it, because the inventory doesn't say a word about it, and it's one of the best pictures we have. Mr. Dalton was talking about it only the other day, and he's a judge of such things, you know. Just look at the keys in the saint's hand,—and then the robes, too, and the glory about his head; it's quite plain who it is meant to represent."

But Gibbins was unaffected by such arguments.

"Well, sir, he *wur* a gen'lemun, warn't he?" he asked, in some surprise at what probably

appeared to him to be a most unorthodox imput-
ation upon St. Peter's private life.

"Yes, I don't suppose anyone would care to
deny that," laughed Arnold. "I suppose the
inventory is right enough, then, and it's my
fault if I don't understand it."

"That's my notion, sir," replied Gibbins with
uncompromising severity. "You see, Mr. Arnold,"
he proceeded, "I allus likes to set down a thing
fair and square jest so fur as I'm sure on it, and
no further. In the matter o' carpets, now, a
Bristle ain't a Kidderminster, neither is a Kidderminster a Bristle, to put it reversely. A good
Kidderminster may be better nor a bad Bristle,
but it ain't my business to say so."

"Very true, Gibbins. 'Portrait of a gentleman'
is safe ; it doesn't rouse any angry feelings. If
you were to say more, you might meet with
opposition, eh ?"

"Ezactly. Folks has different tastes, sir."
Gibbins swelled with the magnitude of his topic.
"What's this 'ere, now ?" he continued, grasping
the arm of his chair. "Me-ogny, to be sure."
He lay back for a moment, gazing fixedly at
Arnold, as though to challenge contradiction.
Then he solemnly rose, and approached the
bureau, which was standing open as usual.
"And this 'ere other bit o' stuff" (striking it
with his hand) "ain't me-ogny at all, neither

ain't it walnut, nor deal, nor rosewood, but jest
simply oak.   An' it don't make no difference
whether you says it's new or old, or whether you
likes it better or wuss for bein' what it is, 'cos
oak it is, and will allus remain, so long as it 'olds
together," and with that he clenched his fist, and
gave the cabinet another thump.

" Hear, hear ; very forcibly put," cried Arnold,
feeling thankful that Gibbins had not selected
china, or any fragile substance,f or his experi-
ments.   "It won't hold together much longer,
though, if you go on banging it about with that
sledge-hammer of yours, my good friend," he
added.

The warning came too late, however ; for the
bailiff was already stooping over the flap of the
bureau, muttering to himself in a perturbed
manner.

" What, knocked a hinge off?   Never mind ;
we'll have the carpenter up to put it to rights,
if we can't manage it between us," and Arnold
looked over Gibbins' shoulder to see the extent
of the damage.

" I dunno what's come to it," said Joshua in
a tone of rueful apology.   " A little knock like
that couldn't 'a busted it open, if it had been all
right afore, could it, sir ? "

" No, my good man, I see what it is ; stand
out of the light."   Arnold pushed back the

sliding panel, and groped within. . . . . Yes,
there was something besides cobwebs. " Here's
another secret for you to keep, Gibbins; what a
splendid amateur detective you are ! "

The treacherous spring had given again, and
allowed the light to stream into the aperture.
" Wants somethink to hold it open," observed the
delighted bailiff; " I'll pop the poker in the crack
now, and go to find what'll do permanent, till we
can find out how it works. Lor, Mr. Arnold,
what a brighter side this 'ere is, to be sure ! "

Arnold cleared the recess of its contents, and
blew the dust off them. There was a bundle of
old letters, a ring-case, and a piece of board, with
a sheet of paper fastened to it with drawing-pins.
He opened the case with trembling fingers. It
was as he expected ; there was nothing inside.
Of course not. His mother must have mislaid
it,—put it here for security, and forgotten it.
Probably she had never needed it, having always
worn the ring. Then after her death—what had
happened to it ? Where had it been ?

But now for the letters. They were those
which had passed between his father and mother
during their short engagement, and he read them
through with reverent care. He had often wondered what sort of people his father and mother
had been. They both died when he was so young
that he retained only a very slight impression of

them personally, and remembered them chiefly by things which were especially associated with them. These newly-discovered letters, therefore, made his mental picture of the writers much clearer than it had ever been. They had not lived to become old,—indeed, the possession of their amorous confidences, together with portraits representing them at about his own present age, led him to think of them almost as absent contemporaries, and rather as brother and sister than as parents. It was a natural consequence of this that he should fall to comparing his lot, so far as it was known to him, with theirs. Apparently there had been no obstacle to their union; they had met, loved, and married. The short romance of their lives was of too subtle and delicate a texture, to judge by their letters, for the handling of novelists and sensation-mongers. Had they any aims which were not satisfied, which it would have been worth living to see accomplished ? There was nothing to tell of any such. Without doubt they had passed their days in rest and quietness together. And then came the greater tranquillity of death.

"He whom the gods love dies young."

There is an alternative, however, which this venerable saw leaves out of account. Some of the scholars in life's great public school are, indeed, born, as it were, into the sixth form, and removed to another sphere at an early age, when they already know as much as the routine of earth can ever teach them. But there are also some lazy young truants whose obstinate perseverance in lagging behind their fellows, and keeping others back by their bad example, is so incorrigible that the patience of the gods (or schoolmasters, as they may be styled for the purposes of the allegory) is worn out at last, and they are deservedly expelled.

One of the letters was almost entirely about the missing ring, and had evidently been written by Arnold's father to accompany this first gift to his betrothed. In it she was adjured to keep the jewel, when not on her finger, along with his letters to her; and her reply, dated on the day which brought her the ring, contained her solemn assurance that she would observe his request. Allusions to the same subject were scattered about their later correspondence, all pointing to the unmistakable conclusion that the discovery of the letters and ring-case together was no accident. But the enigma as to what had become of the contents of the case was more difficult to solve than ever, now that the determination of its owner to leave it with the letters at her death could not be doubted.

Arnold was upon the point of giving it up when his eyes fell upon the piece of board which held the tell-tale fragment of Mr. Rock's rough catalogue. He gazed at the writing for a moment, and then, uttering an exclamation of surprise, carried it to the window for more searching and curious inspection. There was not the faintest effort at disguise about it ; he recognized the hand—half mercantile, half original—at once. Strange ! But when it came to the stamped address,——why, that was even more startling. This connexion between Hiram Rock and the *Tuba Mirabilis* was unexpected enough, but how they had both got mixed up with his (Arnold Robur's) private affairs seemed altogether inexplicable. He loosened the pins, and removed the paper from the board. The other side was a blank.

"Hallo, Gibbins, did you ever see this ? " he called out excitedly, as the bailiff re-entered the library, bringing with him a rudely improvised contrivance for keeping open the sliding panel in the bureau. "He's axed me that afore," soliloquized Joshua; "I know'd as how his head wouldn't never be well agin."

However, he drew out his spectacles with no less deliberation than before, and took in the sheet of paper thoroughly, holding it at every angle, and leaving no point of view untried.

"I ain't seen that one, sir, but me and Mrs. Marchpane burnt a lot of others like it," he observed at length in an unusually decided tone.

"When? where?" asked Arnold eagerly.

"Why, where else should it be but in here, in this very room, arter them chaps as was here cattle-ogging the books had done usin' of it."

"You mean Mr. Rock from Copesbury, don't you? There was no one else here, was there?"

"Not as I knows on," replied Gibbins with stolid composure; 'ceptin' his own man as come over to help him, and that burglar feller what wasn't cotched. I speck *he* must 'a bin loafin' about a good time some'ers where he got a good sight of our goings on. Leastways he couldn't 'a done the thing neater if he had known all the ins and outs o' the place previous; only he didn't reckon as there warn't nothink for him to take, yer see."

It was not Joshua's fault if the topic of the burglary was not familiar in all its details to his gossips. Practice makes perfect, and stories— even bare recitals of facts—are understood to grow more effective with frequent telling. Every time that Gibbins repeated the account of his adventure he realized more fully than before how capable of dramatic treatment were the incidents of that nocturnal alarm in which he himself had played so important a part. Unfortunately, however, he did not begin to recognize this fact till the novelty of the scene had somewhat worn off. Even now, when he thought that a really good chance of recounting the matter from its earliest commencement had arrived, he was cut short just as he was about to launch forth in his most effective manner.

"What was the name of Rock's assistant?" suddenly enquired Arnold.

"Well, sir, I don't rightly know," stammered the bailiff, embarrassed at having to adjust his thoughts to this abrupt change of subject.

"Like as not I never heerd his surname," he went on after a provoking pause. "Leastways I disremembers it, if I did. But, now I comes to reck'lect, I did happen to hear his master a dressin' of him by his fust name, Mr. Arnold, which, as near as I kin jedge—my mem'ry not bein' so good as it wus, and sevril things 'avin' hinterviewed, so to speak, to put it out o' my 'ead"— Here Mr. Gibbins began to waver, and gave indications of being too confused to proceed.

"Was—" suggested Arnold with desperate patience.

"Ed'ard," ejaculated Joshua brightening, and removing the traces of agitation from his brow with a great sigh of relief.

"Edward, h'm." Arnold pondered.

# CHAPTER II.

## CROSS QUESTIONS AND CROOKED ANSWERS.

" Would I were in an alehouse in London! I would give all my
fame for a pot of ale and safety."—*Henry V.*

THERE was practically nothing further for
Arnold to settle with the bailiff, and that honest
philosopher was soon dismissed in a tolerably
cheerful frame of mind.  At all times it is a
pleasant thing to have one's merits duly appreciated, and Joshua now felt that Mrs. Marchpane's
bitter comment on the contents of his skull had
been more than compensated by the acknowledge-
ment of wisdom manifestly implied in the high-
sounding title his master had bestowed on him.
He smiled inwardly—for it must not be supposed that the muscles of his countenance were
allowed to relax—as he marched forth;  his
thoughts, to use the phrase he would probably
have adopted to describe his feelings, were such
as " made his innards feel comfortable-like.'
Presently he paused and addressed the empty
flower-beds.

" Now, for why wur he so set agin my sayin'

it to her? Why? in course, because it wur too good a name for her! Bless you, she's sharp; but, bein' a woman, don't know no better. Wouldn't she jest ha' wondered if she'd heard! Apy—apy—now what was it?" he rubbed his chin in meditation; "apy—ah, that's it, sure enough—apoller-gy fur common sense:" and relapsing into silent self-gratulations the sage went on his way rejoicing.

Meantime Arnold was less agreeably employed. Here were new complications. It was clear enough that Rock and his associate were to be held responsible for the actual removal of the ring; nor was there any longer room for doubt that the farther attempt at robbery was to be laid at their door. Then, the bookseller had said not a word of bringing an assistant. Of course that proved nothing; but at least it tallied with the theory of his guilt. Again, who was this associate? There were two clues only, —the tell-tale fragment of paper bearing the stamp of the office of the *Tuba* and the name Gibbins had caught and reported with so much difficulty, "Edward." So far there did not seem much help towards identifying the culprit. "Edwards are common enough," said Arnold to the book-shelves, as he prepared to fill a pipe which might assist him to a solution of the problem.

But it only needed the audible pronunciation
of the words to set Arnold on the right track.
"Edward" seemed very little use; but "Edwards"
was strikingly suggestive, taken in conjunction
with that stamped paper.

"He looked vicious enough for anything, with
his big beard," mused Arnold, "and he would
have had no difficulty in coming down here if
he'd wanted to. It certainly looks uncommonly
suspicious. Someone from the *Tuba* it must
have been; and someone of sufficient importance
there to use paper with the office stamp on it.
That fits on to Edwards too."

Arnold had only once seen the man he
suspected, and now various circumstances of
that meeting, only half noticed at the time,
recurred to his mind. Edwards had seemed to
find his name familiar; perhaps Rock and he
had already made their preliminary arrangements
then. Again, the newspaper diplomatist had
undoubtedly extracted from Robur a good deal
of information about himself. Everything seemed
to support the view which was now becoming
certainty in our hero's mind, though the evidence,
a piece of stamped paper and a half-remembered
name, was scarcely adequate for conviction by
a jury.

As to Rock's own guilt, on the other hand, the
evidence was much stronger. It was manifest

that the drawer containing the ring-case had been opened while the cataloguing was going on ; and, unless something had been appropriated, so garrulous a gentleman as the bookseller of Copesbury would certainly have mentioned the incident to Gibbins ; yet Gibbins was apparently wholly ignorant of the existence of this secret drawer, nay, had been so struck by the discovery that his habitual melancholy had been relieved by a flash of satisfaction, and he had declared that "here was a brighter side." Arnold chuckled as he thought of the worthy bailiff's air and voice.—Very well: Rock had stolen the ring ; but that being granted, there appeared another difficulty ;—how had Frank got hold of it ? He must have had it from Rock or his colleague ; but what connexion was there between these three reprobates ? Frank's visits to Copesbury had always been a source of mystery to his family ; it made them none the less mysterious that the bookseller had something to do with them, as this ring business clearly showed that he had.

It is curious to observe how often we arrive at right conclusions from quite mistaken premises. Given a problem, we may extract a correct answer, and yet not have a sound line in the process, as the schoolboy who cribs from a key, but has to work out his sum by a method entirely his own, very well knows. If our young friends would only lay to heart the disastrous consequences sometimes entailed by this way of doing things, they would give up their bad habits—or if moral considerations fail to influence them, go the whole hog, and trust to physical pressure to induce their smaller and sharper fellows to let them crib the whole thing. *Verbum Sap.* Robur by a wholly erroneous process had discovered the actual fact that Frank's Copesbury visits had terminated at Mr. Rock's miscellaneous book-store. But the false step, the assumption that his own ring which he had seen on Ursula's finger had been placed there by Frank, though it set him on a right track here, had led him hopelessly and miserably astray on a matter of far more vital importance. But the immediate consequence was that he resolved to interview Mr. Rock without delay.

Then, being in a restless frame of mind, he determined to kill two birds with one stone, clear out of Oakleigh bag and baggage, and escape from the annoyances of the letters and enquiries that were certain to pursue him from Burnport. So he seized an opportunity when Mrs. Marchpane's occupations would ensure her ignorance of his proceedings, bade the bailiff make ready the pony and trap, and in that worthy's company departed to the station.

There Mr. Gibbins, with a parting injunction to his master to "rest upon him" during his absence, left Arnold to follow his own inclinations, and departed homewards in state.

Joshua's mind was of an order which was strongly averse to hurry; there was no proverb more to his taste than "more haste less speed." He seldom gave himself up to obstinate questionings of sense and outward things; unconscious cerebration was his "lay"; but just now he was a little puzzled, and he did not like to own it even to himself, for the confession would be degrading to one of his superior talents; but he would have liked to know what Arnold meant by appearing and vanishing again in this unexpected manner. At the same time he felt that the question was one about which a judicious philosopher should not trouble himself.

Accordingly he assumed an air of Epicurean indifference when he met Mrs. Marchpane that evening at tea-time. The good housekeeper was evidently in a state of perturbation, and was eyeing him with extreme inquisitiveness. Certainly the becoming thing, he felt, would be to let the lady take the lead in asking questions. She did not keep him waiting long.

"Joshua!" she said.

"Mrs. Marchpane, mum?" he replied deferentially.

" Did you see when Mr. Arnold left the house ? "

Joshua leaned back calmly in his chair. " Well, mum, I s'pose I may say,' without doin' a injury to no one, as I did so."

" Did he go to the station ? "

"Seems as I don't jest know if I oughter say, seein' Mr. Arnold hain't left no 'count."

Mrs. Marchpane was upset by these subtle replies. It was obvious that Joshua knew something, but she suspected his silence of being intended merely to enhance his own importance.

" Come, Joshua," she said enticingly, "if the master didn't tell you to hold your tongue, I'm sure I don't see why you shouldn't answer a body. Here's your tea."

The bailiff accepted the tea in silence, and sipped it, but apparently found it too hot. He prepared to follow the simple receipt, much in vogue in humble society, for cooling it by pouring it into his saucer.

" Some more milk, Mr. Gibbins ? " said Mrs. Marchpane.

Gibbins was mollified : partly by the housekeeper's friendly attention to his wants, partly by the polite title she employed to address him.

" Thankee, mum, I will," he responded, avoiding a pedantic regard for grammatical purism. " And," he proceeded slowly, " I dunno as I see no reason why I shouldn't tell you what I knows. Mr. Arnold, he come to me about two o'clock, and he says, ' Get the 'oss an' trap ready,' says he. ' Which 'oss ? ' says I, ' the grey ? ' ' That'll do,' says he. ' Axin' your pardon, sir,' says I, ' but I don't think as he will. You think he's all right,' says I, ' but he ain't. That 'umbuggin' 'oss is wobbly on the 'ocks,' says I. ' Well, then, bring the pony,' says he. ' Werry good, sir,' says I. So I did, and we putt his luggage in the shay, an' druv down to the station together. ' Good-bye, Gibbins,' says he when we'd got there. ' Good-bye, sir,' says I, ' and, if I might ax, where be you agoin' now ? ' ' Into the train,' says he. ' Werry good,' says I, ' an' I 'opes there won't be no accident, though it do seem as if there warn't no brighter side at times, barrin' a-discoverin' of that drawer,' says I ; ' an' while you're away, rest upon me,' I says, an' so I left him."

Mrs. Marchpane had listened to this recital with certain signs of impatience. She seized her opportunity to try and elicit farther information.

" What station did he go to ? " she asked.

Gibbins accomplished the feat of putting himself thoroughly outside a large mouthful of bread and butter, and about half the contents of his tea-cup before making reply.

" Station ? I didn't ax," he said, with no

more sign of excitement than Gallio is reported
to have displayed.

"You didn't find out? and Mr. Arnold gone
off without a word to any one, luggage and all,
and never left so much as an address! What's
to be done with the letters, I should like to
know? Joshua, I'm ashamed of you."

But these taunts did not touch the philosopher,
armed in the "hard-wood and three-fold brass,"
as fourth form boys translate, of conscious merit.
Had Rock been only by to quote the names
of sages who suffered from the tongues (not
to mention the hands) of Xantippes, Mr. Gibbins
could but have been a trifle confirmed in a view
as to the comparative worth of Self and Womankind which was already strongly established in
his own mind.

Joshua, then, received Mrs. Marchpane's re-
proaches with bland imperturbability. He spoke
not, but consumed bread and butter; cheerfully
and undemonstratively, perhaps, but effectively.
Throughout the meal Mrs. Marchpane launched
a series of hits at him, which dropped harmless.
But at last the "reddycule" waxed too warm.
When Mrs. Marchpane hinted that if he had
treated Mr. Rock to such "stupid tongue-tied-
ness" he must have been a dreary companion, he
nearly forgot himself.

"Mrs. Marchpane, mum, if you had heard

them words as Mr. Arnold said to me in the libery yesterday, you wouldn't be a-callin' me in sich-wise. And as for Mr. Rock——" Suddenly the bailiff's face assumed an air of horror, and his jaw dropped.

"Excuse me, mum, but I've an idee," he exclaimed, and precipitately fled.

"You had better make the most of such a rarity," was Mrs. Marchpane's parting shot.

Had Mr. Rock been able to probe the thoughts that were occupying the master of Oakleigh that afternoon he would probably have felt uneasy. But occultism, thought-reading, psychical research, esoteric Buddhism, etc., were to him but meet subjects for the levity of his irreverent vein; he had never even thought seriously about an astral body; and so he sat peacefully at home, unexpectant of approaching storms; his head surrounded indeed by clouds, but only of tobacco smoke. His mind was untroubled by fears of detection. It had hardly occurred to him that the fragment of catalogue might betray him and his confederate; had not Edwards told him that the ring was comfortably out of the way? On this point then he felt safe; Edwards, he imagined, had his eye on both Robur and young Dalton at Burnport: and the only fear that really disturbed him somewhat was that Frank's attempt on Arnold might have been

discovered, and his own connexion with that
exceedingly ill-managed transaction be made
known; but that he regarded as a most unlikely
contingency.

And so it was that when on this Friday afternoon he heard a step in his shop, and descended
to find Arnold Robur awaiting him, he completely mistook that gentleman's object in visiting him, and greeted him with his usual urbanity,
though he was somewhat surprised at his presence
in that neighbourhood.

"Ah! Mr. Robur," quoth he, bowing his unkempt head, and "washing his hands with invisible
soap and imperceptible water," "glad to see you
again, sir.   That is what I have always found in
the course of an experience which extends over
a very considerable number of years—though it
isn't years that make a man old—that when a
customer has once visited my emporium, he is
exceedingly likely to return.   There are few
places to be found so fascinating to those who
know anything of books as an abode like mine.
There was the late Bishop of Copesbury now : a
most learned man, with a fine taste for poetry—
he once came in here by accident to get a fine
old edition of one of the Early Fathers he happened to notice in my window; and by the way,
sir, there are few prelates now-a-days who know
how to value such a book as that.   Well, he

came in, and we had a talk, and I showed him a passage in Augustine he told me he had been looking for a long time and couldn't find; and from that day he was always dropping in to see if I hadn't any fine old vellum-backed editions of Tertullian, and Origen, and other people of that kind, such as would look well in a library. He knew something about the insides of them too, and he used to get quite melancholy now and then over this lax and latitudinarian age, and its ignorance of all genuine theology. Our young men now-a-days, sir, don't seem to care about that sort of thing, and it don't pay to keep books of the kind," said Mr. Rock, finishing up for want of breath, and having also temporarily exhausted his capacity for rapid and effective invention.

Arnold had listened patiently to this long address. He was not practised in diplomacy, and felt very uncertain as to the best method of conducting the business on hand : so he resolved to let his companion talk while he made his preparations for attack. Therefore he sat in silence, confident that Mr. Rock's volubility had only received a momentary check, and that he would go on again directly ; merely picking up a small edition of a classic that lay close beside him. The action was quite sufficient to supply the bookseller with a text for a fresh discourse.

"There now," he exclaimed, "that's the sort
of thing people like now; fancy editions—not
good old folios or quartos, with worm-eaten
backs and big letters inside with *f*'s like f's; such
as the Earl of Widdling used to be so fond
of. Often and often he's said to me, for he was
fond of me in his way, 'Rock, my friend, it's a
sad thing, but these young fellows don't know a
good book when they see it. Look at that book
there now,' and he'd point to something two or
three hundred years old, 'that's worth all the
modern trash. Why, the engraving at the beginning'—they all have wood-cuts at the beginning, you know, sir—'the engraving at the beginning would be cheap at a hundred pounds.
And now here we are, printing off books by the
million in type that's enough to blind a man in
six months,'"—there was no doubt that this was
true enough of the article Arnold held in his
hand,—"and then he would go off into raptures
over a picture of the Muses or Graces, or Lord
knows who. However, he always finished by
buying, which is more than most folks do. They
come in, with their 'Good morning, Mr. Rock,'
and just look round, and pick up a book or two,
and turn over the pages, and say they'll look in
again another day, and then they go. Why, sir,
there was a gentleman came in here the other
day, and spent the best part of an hour among

my books. 'Got Orelli's Horace?' says he after a bit. 'Yes, sir,' said I, and found him a copy. Turned it over a few minutes. 'Don't think I'll take it this morning,' he says. 'Got Lucretius?' says he, after looking round again some while. I forget whose Lucretius it was he wanted, but I had a copy of it. Looked at that a long time. 'Ah, well,' says he, putting it down, 'don't think I'll take that either.' 'Found what you want, sir?' said I, innocently. 'Yes,' said he, 'there were some passages I wanted to compare, and I've done it now.' 'Perhaps you'll use your own books next time instead of mine,' said I. You should have seen his face : he turned the colour of a boiled lobster, and went out without a word."

Mr. Rock began to suffer from exhaustion about this time, and Arnold felt that his remarks were not altogether free from monotony.

"I think," he said, while his companion drew breath, "that if you will continue your confidences in a slightly more private place, it would perhaps be as well. A stranger might come in, and we should find that so disappointing. Besides, it will be more suitable for business, when we do arrive at that stage."

"Not come to purchase to-day, sir? Ah yes, I quite understand. Follow me, sir, and we shall be quite alone—far from the maddening

crowd's ignoble strife, as the poet says. This
way, sir," and Rock conducted his visitor to the
sanctum up-stairs.

Now that it had come to the point, Arnold
hardly knew how to begin. He wanted to convict Rock of his offences and discover his accom-
plices. Rock himself, on the other hand, was
certainly feeling nervous, though he attempted
to conceal the fact. Of course his fears might
be groundless, and Robur's business of the
lucrative, not the annoying order. But this
request for privacy looked suspicious.

Arnold made the first move : tentatively, and
with the air of a man merely making a casual
enquiry.

" Is the sale of secondhand books, varied by
intervals of cataloguing the libraries of the aristocracy, your only occupation in life, Mr. Rock ? "

" What the dickens is he after ? " thought the
venerable bookseller. " Well, sir," he said aloud,
" business does take up most of my time. Re-
creation is for the young, sir ; at my years we
become provident, and keep an eye to the main
chance. But I won't say that, if I had an offer
of lucrative employment of an intellectual character, I mightn't be inclined to give up my
library ; though there are advantages about my
present profession which would weigh pretty
heavily against making any change. Of course,

as to undertaking temporary work, that depends on the season, and the cash. No doubt," said the ancient one, "I should manage to enjoy life under less favourable circumstances; a philosopher is always happy—but then there's no denying that philosophy is easier to practise on a comfortable income. That's what the Marquis of Muddington thought. He was a great philosopher, and wrote books about the Lord knows what, and how the wise man was satisfied with bread and cheese; but when his son dropped something like half a million in racing debts his language was simply awful. 'Why, father, what's become of your philosophy?' says the youngster, who was a good-tempered, hearty sort of chap, and kept the tenth commandment splendidly,—for you see there's no need to covet your neighbours' goods if you can get them to put their names to a bill. 'Where's your philosophy, dad?' says he. 'D—n philosophy,' says the Marquis; 'if the estate wasn't entailed, I'd cut you off with a shilling.' 'Sorry to hear you say that,' says the other; 'haven't the books been selling then?' There wasn't much love lost between the two, though. But as I was saying, there isn't much to be done besides selling my books just now—which is more than the Marquis ever did, by the way," said Mr. Rock with a chuckle.

"Ah, yes," said Arnold, who had seated himself, and gazed contemplatively at his companion
during this oration : "I fear you misunderstand
me.   I mean that I want to know what you have
on sale besides books."

"On sale, sir ?  Nothing else but some few newspapers," replied Rock, puzzled by Arnold's tone.

"Really ?   But you have some customers
whose tendencies are scarcely literary, who still
seem to have found your society as attractive as
the book-lovers."

"You compliment me greatly, sir : I always
did fancy that versatility was one of my characteristics ; that was what the late Duke of
Ditchling used to say to me.  'Rock, my boy,'
he would say "——

"The late Duke was no doubt a most affable
person, Mr. Rock ; and dispensed the favour of
his regard with surprising freedom for so staunch
a hater of the Democracy.   But our present
business has no connexion with him, as you are
probably aware.   Kindly make an effort to keep
the conversation a trifle nearer home."

Rock was unaccustomed to this sort of treatment : interruption did not suit him ; least of
all did he expect it from Arnold, whom he had
classified somewhat hurriedly as guileless—not
to say green.   He was greatly put out, and it
took him some moments to recover the shock.

Arnold's confidence was increased, though he had never felt much doubt. He resolved to make a bold move, and risk the blunder.

" I am hardly to blame for our taking so long in coming to the point," he said ; " we have been wandering round among the pecrage a trifle too long. I want an explanation of your connexion with a gentleman who lives near me : you understand ? "

" Oh, Lord, it's coming," said Rock to himself ; " how on earth am I to get out of it ? We'll try a facer. I've had nothing to do with Mr. Dalton," he said, looking stolidly at Arnold.

Robur smiled. " Thanks," he said. " Out of thine own mouth, etcetera. How do you know I was referring to Mr. Dalton ? "

The bookseller's countenance fell. He had made an awful blunder, for which the confusion into which he had been thrown by Arnold's attack was responsible.

" Why—why—who else is there ? " he stammered.

" That, my friend, is not the question. You wouldn't have named Mr. Dalton, but for the relation between you which is an established certainty,—and was so before, though you have now been good enough to confirm it. It is really a pleasant surprise to find you so ready to commit yourself."

"Well then, I won't deny it, though the young gentleman asked me to keep it quiet, because he said the governor wouldn't like it."

"Possibly the governor wouldn't," said Arnold dryly. "But our account isn't settled by your little admission, Mr. Rock. However, it is so far a comfort to know that Mr. Frank Dalton's peculiarities of conduct are not altogether an original growth. It would be interesting to learn the precise proportion of his natural inclinations to your external influence."

"He's found out all about it," thought the bookseller: "the young fool has been saying that we egged him on to shoot: shouldn't wonder if he had said he got the pistol from me, confound him. And I don't see how to deny all that Mack told him. We'll make an effort to persuade this party that it was all his own idea, and we tried to dissuade him."

He proceeded to address Robur apologetically, summoning his invention into play again.

"Well, it's hard on a man to have a young fool's misdoings piled on his shoulders; but it's the way of the world. Why, even at school I remember it was the same, and I used to get licked for the other boys' mischief."

The slight smile of incredulity awakened on Arnold's features by this statement was justifiable; for Mr. Rock did not suggest one of those characters who get all their neighbours' kicks, and not even their own half-pence; but it rather irritated the bookseller.

"Why," he said, "you may laugh; but I've been a victim all my life. And now in my old age, to have it put down to me because Mr. Frank Dalton goes about the country breaking the law and playing the fool,—it's rather too much of a good thing. Perhaps he's been putting it down to Mack—I shouldn't wonder."

Arnold was certainly rather mystified by this harangue. Was Rock trying to make him believe that Frank was responsible for the robbery, and was indeed the actual perpetrator? No doubt that was the original idea which Robur had had in his mind before the fragment of catalogue was discovered, but it was simply absurd to put that interpretation on it now. Frank would never have come over to Oakleigh while the cataloguing was going on; and even if he had, Gibbins would inevitably have mentioned it. On the other hand, the close of the bookseller's speech sounded very like a confirmation of his suspicions about Edwards, who had been called Mack by Mr. Bloss, as he remembered. And Edwards could hardly have been assisting at Oakleigh in that mysterious manner without some mischievous intent. No, Mr. Rock was

making a very futile move, if that was the aim
of his remarks.

"You don't suppose," he said, "that I am
going to show you my hand, and tell you how
much I know. I will go so far as to say that I
hold the master cards, and it will take very good
play on your part and very bad play on mine for
you to win. I don't think folks will be wise who
lay on your success."

The interesting thing about this discussion
was that the speakers were at cross purposes.
Rock thought only of Frank's shot at Arnold;
Arnold had no suspicion of Rock's complicity in
that little business, having connected him with
Frank solely in the matter of the ring; while
the other again, entirely ignorant of Arnold's
knowledge of the whereabouts of the ring, which
had never been in Frank's hands at all, had no
notion that the robbery was the subject which
was engrossing his interlocutor's attention; and
naturally he was without the slightest conception
of the extent of Robur's information.

"Confound it, sir," he said dolorously, "the
boy must have been telling you a pack of lies.
I own that I knew something about it, and so
did Mack" (Rock had assumed, as he could
hardly help doing, that "Mack" and he had
alike been accused); "and perhaps some of the
stories he heard here, before he told us what he

CROSS QUESTIONS AND CROOKED ANSWERS. 43

meant to do, may have excited him a bit; for
Mack's experience is wide, and he likes to talk
about the things he's seen, and never dreamed
the young ass would look at them in the light
he did : but we both told him he was a fool, and if
you'd heard the way I slated him when he told
me what he'd done, for I hadn't believed he
would really do it, you wouldn't talk to an old
man like me in the way you've been doing, sir ; "
and his voice dropped into a mournful whine,
while his attitude betokened limpness of an
exaggerated character.

Arnold rose and stood before the fire, with
his hands in his pockets, looking at Rock. Now
when you argue it is no use for both parties to
stand up. You cannot dominate a man whose
head is on the same level as your own. If the
argument is of an exciting character, perhaps
the most effective plan is to lounge in a chair,
while your opponent stands up : there is an
air of easy mastery about this attitude which is
likely to throw him into confusion or else to
irritate him—both most desirable results, if
your object is simply to win. But if you find
this arrangement impracticable, make *him* sit
down and stand up yourself; which, if once
you have made him nervous, is very nearly as
good. In short, as long as you are on the defensive, you score by being casual ; but for hard

hitting, it pays better to assume the imperative manner.

Our hero acted on this principle. He lounged, and adopted a bland demeanour till he had made quite sure of his man; now he was going to change his tactics.

"Mr. Rock," he said, "you have now taken to talking pure nonsense, which I assure you is not of the slightest use. I am not going to discuss how far it was you and how far it was our friend from the *Tuba* that was responsible for this affair; at any rate, your share is certain; and between you, in addition to your other pleasing displays of character, you have managed to do Frank Dalton a considerable amount of harm; and you will not be surprised to hear that a good deal of annoyance has resulted to me. For reasons of my own, you may be pleased to learn, I do not mean to come down heavily on him: you may be less pleased to learn that I do not propose letting you off with equal ease. I have not made up my mind what to do with you yet; but I warn you that you are under my thumb. You are watched, so that escape will be impossible, and any attempt in that direction will remove all chance of gentler treatment."

Arnold gazed down on the bookseller, who throughout this speech was growing limper and more limp in attitude, more puzzled and miserable in expression.

" I don't know how you found out that he came from the *Tuba*," he groaned, when Robur paused, " and I do think you're very hard on a man just for talking to a fool of a boy who goes and doesn't even know how to do a thing right when he sets about it. There now, I tell you, it was just nothing but some cock-and-bull story of Edwards',—it's no use calling him Mack now, since you know all about it,—of the way he'd served somebody he had found to be an enemy. Of course it was all invented, and he had never shot him ; but it excited young Dalton, and off he went and got a pistol ; and you know the rest. But I swear we neither of us meant matters to end as they did ;" which was true enough : Mr. Rock had meant Arnold to receive his quietus.

Had the old gentleman been watching Arnold's face instead of gazing miserably at his boots while he made his confession, he might have stopped half way. But he was labouring under a complete delusion as to the whole drift of the young man's words, and fancying his connexion with Frank's escapade to be the subject under discussion, he made up his mind that the best way to get comparatively merciful treatment was to make a clean breast of the whole concern.

But to Robur his words were a revelation of

hitherto wholly unsuspected criminality. He saw at once that Rock had misunderstood him throughout the dialogue, and while his admission of intimacy with Edwards left it beyond a doubt that the newspaper diplomatist was most justly suspected of partnership in the actual theft of the ring, it was now also perfectly clear that these companions in crime of one kind were companions also in farther crime of an equally serious character. There was a crumb of comfort too in the thought that Frank Dalton's own brain had not originated the idea of assassination ; while these two scoundrels, even if they had not, as he was now strongly inclined to think, directly instigated the attempt, had beyond question known of it beforehand, and had yet made no effort to frustrate it. Probably too, he thought, the ring had been passed on to the unconscious Frank in order to bring him under suspicion, on the presumption that the relations of Arnold to the family at Beau Séjour would prevent anything in the shape of a legal scandal ; and he could not help smiling at the thought of this ingenious application to practical life of the nursery game of " hunt the ring." He stood for some moments in silent contemplation.

Rock, receiving no reply, looked up at him, and was slightly encouraged by the amused expression on his face.

"I'm very sorry, sir," he ventured to say, "very sorry to see you marked like that. But young Dalton was such a blamed young fool, sir."

Arnold awoke from his reverie. "I really think you're right," said he. "He was a blamed young fool, as you say, to take to such guides, philosophers, and friends as you and Edwards. But a young fool doesn't hold a candle to an old fool, when the latter is really bent upon showing his weak points. You made a delightful slip at the very beginning of our conversation, my friend; you made another when you named Edwards; but the very biggest slip of all was that charmingly candid confession at the end. I knew that you had some connexion with Dalton; but until the moment you were seized with such deep contrition I had no notion of your share in setting this cheerful scar on my forehead. Now I know that, in addition to the theft of my ring, and farther happily unsuccessful attempts at robbing me in conjunction with our common friend Mack, or Edwards, or whatever other name he goes by, of the *Tuba*, which theft was practically proved before, though your remarks have made it entirely instead of nearly certain; in addition to this, it is you I have to thank for something like a month's ill-health, and a permanent scar. Your *naïveté* is touching; so touching that I will defer your punishment for a few days. Good morning. By the way, you seem to be suffering from these discoveries,— what has become of your philosophy?" and with this parting shot Arnold departed.

Rock rose and watched him out of the door with anguish on his brow. "Damn philosophy," he said, unconsciously quoting the reply of the Marquis of Muddington, as he shook his fist at the door.

Then, with perspiration on his forehead, he dropped in an invertebrate heap on to a chair.

"Devil take it!" he said, and gasped: "what will my partner do to me for this?"

# CHAPTER III.

## SQUIRES AND DAMES.

" For indeed I knew
Of no more subtle master under heaven
Than is the maiden passion for a maid,
Not only to keep down the base in man,
But teach high thought, and amiable words,
And courtliness, and the desire of fame,
And love of truth, and all that makes a man."
*Idylls of the King.*

THE Daltons' sojourn at Burnport was a critical epoch in Frank's life. It was a period of transition for him from the lowest abyss of ineptitude —if there can be an abyss in anything so shallow —towards the higher level of sober mediocrity. Ursula's society during the last week of the time which he had the good fortune to spend within easy reach of her could not fail to affect him wholesomely, as soon as the first gush of exaggerated despair lost its not unpleasing effervescence, and grew stale and vapid. After all, he thought, there really was no reason why he should give up her company before he was obliged ; while his present mournful seclusion, though it might be dignified, was most assuredly becoming a " beastly bore." Besides, he had tried sulking in her presence, and knew by sad experience that this method was unlikely to occasion her the acutest remorse : it would probably only have the result of making her avoid him, a contingency before which his hardihood completely broke down. Frank was wise in his generation : if one cannot secure the best, why should one relinquish the second best ? he unconsciously argued. He could not hope to marry Ursula, but that did not prevent him from seeking to cultivate her acquaintance. His very intention made a perceptible difference in our juvenile friend, and it is scarcely necessary to remark that there could have been few changes for the worse in his case.

Not that his enchantress could at once transform a brutish yokel into a high-souled cavalier. Ignorant and clumsy young Dalton still remained, but there was something undeniably new in his disposition.

Perhaps his chance of coming to such senses as had not lapsed away from him through disuse was not so bad as it might have been. No one could accuse him, for instance, of being a modish dilettante, nor was he a prey to the enervating influence of certain modern developments of Art.

Not being a person for whom the niceties of scholarship or the intricacies of versification had ever possessed even a passing interest, he did not forthwith set about composing a quantity of dolefully self-conscious stanzas on such classical themes as " Faithless Phyllis," or " Lesbia's left me in the lurch ; " by means of which pleasing allegorical device the symmetrical throes of the poet's voluble chagrin have received ere now no inconsiderable relief.

Ursula on her way back from her drawing-class one morning met her foiled admirer looking strangely dishevelled, his garments and general appearance giving indubitable proofs that he had lately been through a good deal of physical exertion. He raised a very battered hat, which had completely lost its pristine elegance of out-line, to say nothing of hue, and panted awkwardly enough,—

" I've just—been—out—all night—in—a fish-ing-smack,—and—my hands—are all over tar and stuff." Here he made a desperate attempt to improve their condition by wiping them on his yet more filthy trousers, the result being such as to make him look more harassed and ashamed of himself than ever.

Ursula was thoroughly surprised. She would hardly have recognized him, he looked so—well, almost honest and pleasant, in spite of his

unkempt and odoriferous condition. A happy
inspiration prompted her to be generous, and
not decline his fishy overtures. So with laudable
readiness she set about administering a little
friendly encouragement to the humbled youth.

"You look quite famished, Mr. Dalton. What
an adventurous time you must have had. Weren't
you half perished with cold? Let me walk back
with you; I've been sitting still for hours; and
I want to see Grace."

Never was sympathy better timed. Perhaps
Frank had never felt the need of it before.
Anyhow, the tiny spark of manliness in him
kindled at her words, and the kindly confidence
they implied. Certainly Ursula had something
of that "wonderful way" with her which is
traditionally associated with the name of Father
O'Flynn. The combined novelties of hunger
and unmixed sea-air had quickened the young
gentleman's perceptions.

"It wasn't so very cold, Miss Lorton," he
replied gratefully, taking the outside of the path
by some docile instinct. "We had tarpaulins
and coats, and that sort of thing: besides, there
was plenty to do, and I managed to keep pretty
warm, and didn't feel a bit seasi—queer, you
know."

There was a pathetic touch about the substitu-
tion which more than atoned for its squeamish-

ness. Viewed as a sign that Frank was not
altogether without a germ of consideration for
other people's feelings, it sounded promising.

" I dare say you'll find it has done you all the
good in the world when you are rested," said
Ursula, smiling ; " I'm so glad you went."

It was worth risking a cold to hear this. "·I've
a good mind to go again to-night," cried Frank
stoutly.

" No, no," laughed the girl ; " you've shown
you can do it, and that's enough, unless you can
really be of help. But tell me all about it, and
what you did and saw," she added with feminine
alertness, perceiving that he was only to be made
manageable by dint of careful discipline.

Then Frank broke out into a long ungram-
matical rigmarole detailing the circumstances of
his escapade, in the course of which he fell into
as many logical traps, and perpetrated as many
solecisms as would fill a small handbook, to say
nothing of a persistent tautology that made
Ursula's flesh creep,—if it is possible for a young
lady to experience so uncompromising a sensation.

Nevertheless she heard him with more pleasure
than annoyance ; and when at length he paused
for breath, she experienced a most unfeminine
inclination to slap him on the back.

" Really I'm surprised Mrs. Dalton let you
go," she said, after complimenting him again

upon his performance; and her voice rippled
with half-mischievous merriment.

" I didn't tell her," said Frank; "you won't
either, will you ? " he added in a tone of confiding
entreaty; "'cos there'd be no end of a row if
she found out, and I don't mean her to if I can
help it."

Can anything palliate Ursula's heedless im-
propriety ? She actually promised to aid and
abet him in this treacherous design.

" D' you know, Miss Lorton, I want awfully to
ask your advice about something," was Frank's
next remark, uttered with husky desperation.

" Can't you find someone better to advise
you ? " she asked a little anxiously, for she could
not help fearing that he might be misguided
enough to repeat his flattering offer. " I'm not
sure of advising you right," she went on, "and
perhaps I should be unsympathetic, and say
something that would hurt your feelings."

Frank hung his head. He understood the
hint,—who can be quite bereft of insight when
he can admire ?—and he may have been conscious
that his feelings deserved to be hurt.

" I—I—it has nothing to do with you, Miss
Lorton ; only I thought—"

" Yes," responded Ursula, promptly coming to
his relief, " I should like to do anything for you
in a friendly way."

Thus encouraged, Frank proceeded at once to put his case.

"Suppose you had done something awfully bad to a fellow,—a person, I mean,—and he knew it, and just let you off without saying anything about it; at least, of course *you* couldn't have done it, you know, but suppose I had." He turned aside and gasped.

"I suppose you mean a personal injury," said Ursula quietly, "no matter what; and the injured person, discovering his injurer,—though he knows how it all happened, and that the mischief was not done unintentionally, or through an accident,—hushes it up to screen the injurer, and never betrays him to human justice."

Frank nodded; it was all he could do. Something of that dreadful faintness came over him again. He tottered to one of the covered seats which was close by, and sat down. He knew it must look strange; but Ursula seated herself beside him without a word.

"Please don't mind," he said, as soon as he could speak. "I'm so tired, and we can talk better here. Yes, suppose he,—the person, you know,—don't take any notice, and goes on the same as before."

Ursula folded her arms firmly as she replied, "The injurer ought to go to him instantly, and implore his forgiveness, besides begging him to take the fullest reparation possible. No time must be lost."

" But suppose it has been lost."

" So much the worse. Then the sooner the wrong-doer confesses, and asks for forgiveness, the better."

" Won't writing do as well ? " moaned Frank.

" Certainly not," said Ursula ; " there is nothing to be risked by it in this case, and it would be more cowardly than doing nothing at all."

Her companion hid his face. He was quivering from head to foot. The girl turned pale ; her sympathy made her dread vaguely some terrible revelation. But she never wavered. True to her sense of duty, her very womanliness kept her from flinching. Bravely she set her face to encounter the seductive weakness which tempted her to spare him, and scorned the momentary pleasantness of ruinous counsels. No enemy is so bad as a false friend. So she persevered with all the courage of her pure motives.

" How could any one go through life with the thought of a wrong once committed, and never even partially atoned for, weighing the heart down ? Vain regret is worse than useless, Frank ; it is a perpetual disease that slowly eats away your happiness, making you infirm

and worn-out before your time. And yet its
attacks are never too violent to be borne without flying to the only remedy that can be
trusted. For the remedy itself seems painful,
—more painful, indeed, every time the sufferer
thinks of it,—and so it is put off, till in the end
the miserable man dies, and the rest is beyond
his power."

Ursula spoke slowly and considerately. The
words would not come all at once, and she was
anxious not to miss the mark either above or below.

The boy was gazing at her now spell-bound.

" Yes, it is hard," she said, interpreting his
look ; " I too know something of its hardness.
No one is ready enough to confess his or her
faults, and sometimes I think I must be worse
than most people in that way."

Frank gave a gulp. " I'll do it," he exclaimed,
clenching a pair of greasy fists, " the very first
chance I get I'll do it. It makes it easier, somehow, hearing you talk about it," he went on,
a faint flush of determination beginning to
appear in his cheeks. " And then your saying
you've felt things like it, that helps a lot. But
oh, you can't know how dreadful it is to have
done what I mean."

" At any rate," pleaded Ursula, " that ought to
make it easier to show your repentance. People
sometimes have to do things quite as unpleasant

without any stings of conscience to help them.
Surely your case is not so hard as theirs. Besides,
if you have been forgiven already in spite of your
silence, it is not very likely that any expression of sorrow on your part will be harshly
rejected."

"I don't know," he replied doubtfully.

They sat silent for an interval, watching the
sea as it surged and thundered upon the beach
below. A solitary sea-gull wheeled about in the
air above their heads, or descended to skim the
surface of the incoming tide. The wind blew
in keen gusts from the land, making the un-
harvested deep hoary with numberless streaks
of foam, as Father Neptune's locks will sometimes turn to grey from hyacinthine in a single
night. From their sheltered position, however,
they were able to contemplate this cheerless
scene without actual discomfort, and remained
mute as two lovers for many minutes, oblivious
to the glances of the passers-by, who were to
be pardoned if they somewhat misjudged the
relation between the pair.

The prospect, combined with the not in-
harmonious flow of her own thoughts, might
have continued to divert Ursula's attention from
all else, had not Frank, on whose raw fibre
tension of any sort was an unaccustomed strain,
opened his lips to repeat—

" I'll do it every bit just as you say, if only you'll forgive me."

This was startling. "How am I to forgive you when you have never done me any harm ?" she asked.

" I can't explain it any better without telling you all about it," said Frank disconsolately. " I never intended to do you any harm, as you say, but I may have done so all the same, you know, without meaning. But promise to forgive me if things turn out like this,—for indeed I'd have shot myself before injuring you, only I didn't know it then,—and I'll go straight for ever afterwards, I swear I will."

Ursula was mystified. However, she was anxious that Frank should not make her accessory to his misdeed, whatever it was,—as he would infallibly have done if she had allowed him to go on blurting out clumsy hints. She did not want to know the facts of the case, and he had already told her everything that was material to it. The utmost she could do now, therefore, was to give him the assurance for which he asked ; and she did so, inwardly pitying the confusion of his ideas, as it seemed to her. Then she rose from the seat, and led the way to the house where the Daltons were staying.

Only Mrs. Dalton was at home, and her son

found to his intense relief that she had but just left her bed-room, as she was suffering that morning from the interesting hallucination that something was the matter with her. For this reason, she sent word, she regretted that her condition rendered her inaccessible to Miss Lorton. Ursula was not sorry to part with her worshipper, who slipped up-stairs stealthily to change his raiment before foraging for victuals.

Nevertheless, as she walked away she was filled with gladness that this chance of doing a real service for someone had not been missed. The embarrassment of the interview being over, she could look back upon it with unmixed satisfaction.

A few days back she would not have behaved so feelingly. But she had begun to know trouble on her own account, and thus she was prepared to listen and advise more tenderly as well as more judiciously when Frank sought to impart his woes to her. She liked the boy for humbling himself as he had done, and not nursing his wounded dignity any longer. By taking this step he occupied a better place in her estimation than she had supposed to be possible. Why had he not consulted Arnold Robur while he was still at Burnport? Once or twice in the course of their conversation she had thought of asking Frank that question, but something prevented

her. That Robur was on very intimate terms
with two members at least of the Dalton family
there could be no doubt. He always behaved as
though he were Mr. Dalton's son and Grace's
eldest brother; but Frank he seemed to make a
rule of avoiding, while no one ever got beyond a
waterish kind of acquaintance with Mrs. Dalton,
—perhaps because there was no footing beyond
to get to. After all it was scarcely surprising
that Robur should feel little interest in such an
unlicked cub as Frank had hitherto been.

The invalid's sudden flight was more perplex-
ing. Aunt Joan had evidently been much worried
about it, though she tried to conceal the fact for
some unknown reason. Grace too was as much
in the dark as her friends, and could only tell
them that a letter had arrived from Oakleigh
which afforded practically no explanation of the
writer's strange conduct in going off without
saying good-bye to any of them. All that could
be gathered for certain was Arnold's intention
not to remain at home (so said Grace) ; he was
going away immediately to pay some visits, and
by this time all clue to his whereabouts had been
lost.

Grace, indeed, was more confounded than anyone, except Miss Joanna, by the turn things had
taken. Being the only two persons who knew
anything about Arnold's hopes, they might have

derived mutual support in the emergency from
an exchange of confidence. But their eyes were
blinded, and, though they were neither of them
suspicious or distrustful by nature, there did not
seem to be any justification for either telling the
other what she knew. Grace, supposing the ring
which Ursula now wore to have been given to her
by Arnold, had been upon the point of congratulating him on his success when his departure
destroyed this premature hypothesis. Speculate
as she might, however, she could not think of
any other to suit.

Ursula wore the ring upon the third finger of
the left hand, on which particular digit such an
ornament became at once a highly suggestive
symbol, according to Grace's old-fashioned ideas.
Now it was impossible to suppose that Arnold
had a successful rival of whose very existence
they all were ignorant. If such was the case,
what could there be to prevent Miss Joanna
from informing her friends the Daltons, especially when she allowed her niece to wear
so conspicuous a token? Upon these grounds
Grace's bewilderment was not unreasonable.
Had there been any valid excuse for absenting
himself under such peculiar circumstances, an
excuse not connected with this entanglement,
Arnold would surely not have neglected to
mention it in his letter. No; whatever it was

that had driven him away, it was clearly something not to be explained without taking them all into his confidence; and this conclusion landed Grace back once more in her apparently hopeless muddle.

As for Joanna, she was not one whit less badly off than the unknown sharer of her suspense. Equally unable to imagine the cause of the young man's defection, she was plagued by a suggestion of her fears, a morbid fancy which she was constantly endeavouring to stifle, that it had something to do with the appearance of Ursula's father upon the scene. It seemed to her an odd coincidence that the two things should have occurred so near together. And yet she could not believe that her opinion of Arnold was erroneous, or that any discovery of events relating to her darling, over which the girl herself could never have had the least control, would make him draw back and renounce the love which he professed to feel for her. No man would choose an unconvicted felon for a father-in-law if he could help it; but the moral characteristics of the beloved one's family do not usually enter into the calculations of any but the most cautious lovers,—people who can only by a wild stretch of language be called lovers at all,—and Arnold had seemed ardent enough. He had deliberately tried to rouse the girl's susceptibility,

without considering the contingencies that might
arise, and about which Joanna had more than
once dropped guarded hints to him.   To retrace
his steps at this juncture would be a piece of
despicable treachery, even supposing his progress
towards earning Ursula's affection to have been
small.   He should have weighed the consequences
of his actions before, and arrived at an accurate
knowledge of his own mind then, if he ever
meant to do so.

But Joanna's heart was too warm and true to
harbour so evil a suspicion for more than the
passing moment.   Besides, how could he know
anything about Lorton or his unsavoury antecedents ?

The supposition was manifestly improbable.
So she determined to wait a little longer, and
then write to Arnold for an explanation, if he
failed to offer one in the mean time.   She refused to allow herself to mistrust him, and tried
to cloak her anxieties under a moderately cheerful
demeanour.

There was another person, however, whose
concern in this affair was more immediate than
Grace and Aunt Joan could be expected to guess.
Frank was the less innocent than ignorant stum-
bling-block over which most of the remaining
actors in the little drama came to grief.   Not
that he felt them tripping up against him, any

more than they knew against whom or what they
were bruising their shins. Nor did he affect to
feel any particular surprise at the intelligence
that Arnold had gone back to Oakleigh beyond
what was conveyed in the terse commentary of
" Doosed rum move." His was one of those careless, trustful minds which forbear on principle,
or for lack of it, to enquire too closely into the
nature of things. So the matter did not weigh
long upon his spirits ; and as for considering
himself to be in the least responsible for Robur's
freakish eccentricity, he did not so much as
trouble his head to think whether there was any
cause for it at all. Moreover, he had a large
repast of other mental food to assimilate and
digest just at present.

In the first place, the naked fact stared him
broadly in the face that he had not fascinated
Ursula as he had expected. This took him the
best part of a day—the day on which he found
it out—to comprehend, and, as it were, masticate
thoroughly. That disposed of, reflections as to
whether his failure could by the remotest possibility be attributable to his own fault, and not
to conscious demerit on her part, occupied all
his powers of analysis and casuistry till the
evening came when he met her again, with the
result of forming a shadowy impression that the
singularly ungraceful close of that negotiation

on the beach was not the only occasion in his life when he had cut a rather sorry figure.

The impression thus formed showed a tendency to solidify, which was fortunately confirmed by an opportune talk with Grace, whose views on the subject were of a more definite character than his own. Perhaps the course of events had sharpened his perceptions a little, for he certainly gathered no very inaccurate notion of Arnold's feelings towards Ursula from his sister's remarks, while at the same time he recognized that Grace had never been in love with him herself. His crime was thus deprived of the only pretext which could be urged for it; and if it was due to his moral instability that he committed the act, hopes seemed to be held out from the same quarter that his bitterness against his enemy would not long outlive the excuse for it. Without saying anything to Grace he resolved to seek Ursula's advice, and abide by it. The thought that he might have inflicted an injury upon her through her lover did not strike him till he was actually unburdening his soul to this sweet confessor, when it had the wholesome effect of deepening his contrition. His confusion made him beg incoherently for her forgiveness, as though she already knew Arnold's passion, and reciprocated it. But prophetic utterances have 'before now sounded incoherent to the hearers;

and Frank's words had a significance, though she did not understand it.

At this stage of affairs who should present himself at Burnport but Paston. He came one Saturday to see a patient whom he had sent down to the seaside for a change after a dangerous illness, and having discharged his professional duties repaired to the hotel at which Robur was in the habit of staying to announce his intention of remaining with his friend over the Sunday. He had purposely abstained from writing beforehand to warn the other of his visit, as he felt certain of finding him still in the place, and wanted to give him a surprise. He was, therefore, considerably taken aback when he learnt that the hotel authorities knew nothing of Mr. Robur later than the fact that he paid his bill and departed three days before.

" Perhaps you know Mr. Dalton, sir," said the landlord. For it was not one of those mighty grand hostelries, which satisfy the requirements at once of an increased population and an enlightened taste, where the attendants preserve an exterior as impassive and uninviting as the stucco covering of its cheap brickwork. " I think Mr. Dalton is still staying at Burnport, sir," said the landlord; " but we'll soon see. William, the *Advertiser*. Mr. Robur came to us from them, you know, sir, and they can tell you all about him. He said he should feel more at home and independent here as soon as he was able to look after himself without any help. Ah, here you are now ;" and he pointed to the Daltons' address in the paper. *" Mr. and Mrs. Dalton, Miss Dalton, Mr. F. Dalton.* It's close by, sir. Turn to the left, and keep straight on in front of the sea. Wish you good day, sir."

Paston was received with open arms by all the members of the family except Frank, and was immediately asked for news about Arnold. A smart fire of cross questions and answers followed, the upshot being that each of the party found that he or she knew as much about the matter as the others, which amounted to very little indeed. Whereupon, at Mr. Dalton's suggestion, they were fain to partake heartily of lunch ; for wonder is an exceedingly appetizing emotion.

Paston soon began to find the society of the old gentleman and his daughter so far from distasteful that he did not resist with much energy the pressure which they put upon him to induce him not to hurry away from Burnport. His anxiety about his absent friend was not to be appeased by a fruitless expedition to Oakleigh. One of the servants from Beau Séjour, sent over only the day before to make enquiries, had found

Mrs. Marchpane in great grief because her master was again " a wanderer upon the face of the earth," as she Biblically expressed it. She did not even know his address. He had taken the opportunity to disappear while she was out ; and Gibbins, who took him to the station, thought he was going back to Burnport, " and so between them they've just managed to make one big mess of the whole concern," concluded Mr. Dalton, puckering up his eyebrows a good deal as he replenished Paston's plate. His serenity was, however, restored to some extent on Grace's asking demurely whether he did not think that a letter addressed to Cupar would have a good chance of finding Arnold.

Grace could not help feeling drawn towards Paston. The doctor was such a big, fatherly person, and gave you the idea of being so much older than he really was. He was devoted to his friend, and, like his friend, got on well with Grace's father ; that was always a crucial test with her of masculine worth.

" Don't some friends of yours live here ? " enquired Paston innocently, after some pre-liminary conversation upon the beauties of the neighbourhood. Grace and he were alone ; Mr. Dalton was taking his nap, Mrs. Dalton her " Siesta,"—a practice in which she was beginning to follow Miss Hilda's lead, — while Frank

studiously kept out of the way for reasons of
his own.

"You mean the Miss Blunsdens, and their
niece Ursula Lorton, I suppose. We'll go round
to tea there this afternoon, and take you with
us. Yes, they're great friends of ours,—and of
Arnold's too. Miss Joanna Blunsden is charming; I expect you'll quite fall in love with her,
though she's not exactly young and lovely, you
know," and Grace took a bundle, wrapped
up in a voluminous silk handkerchief, out of a
work-basket by her side, and unrolled it.

"Ah," ejaculated Paston quietly, pausing
afterwards, as if he were considering some
symptom before making up his mind what to
prescribe.

"But that doesn't signify a bit," he went on,
referring to Grace's remark that personal charms
formed no part of Miss Joanna's attraction.
"For instance, a man's own sisters may be
perfect sylphs and houris to behold, and yet he
may conceivably find their absence less irksome
than their presence. Of course he must be a
brute to do it," he added apologetically, "but
I mean such cases have been known."

"People so seldom see anything in the members
of their own families," said Grace, taking some
work out of the bundle, and wrapping it up
again. "Brothers and sisters, I dare say, often

seem stupid and ugly, and altogether uninterest-
ing to each other, when strangers may think
quite differently about them."

The doctor smiled. "And, contrariwise, they
may be amiable enough in each other's sight,
but loathsome in everybody else's, I suppose,"
he rejoined. "My illustration was a bad one,
because I wasn't thinking of those miserable
beings who despise everything that they happen
to be familiar with, but of tolerably decent folks
whose sense of beauty is so mixed up with their
notion of what is good and right that they can't
separate the two things if they would."

"Well, I've heard Arnold declare that he's
seen Miss Joanna look positively beautiful sometimes," said Grace; "I suppose that's something
like what you mean; but I think it's going a
little far to talk so. People might not understand you, and quiz."

Paston shrugged his broad shoulders. "Your
plea is not a very strong one, I think," he
replied straightforwardly. "The quizzer generally gives chances of having the tables turned
on him beautifully by a bold and wary quizzee.
But perhaps I ought to consider the feelings
of others more than I do."

"Oh, it isn't that," remarked Grace airily;
"but I'm so terribly afraid of ridicule, you
know."

Could she only have known that the failing was one which she shared in common with the profound Gibbins! But this consolation was denied to her, and Paston evinced scant sympathy on this point.

"I can admire indifference to all that kind of thing in others," said Grace, pursuing the subject; "but that doesn't seem to cure me a bit. There's Ursula, now — Miss Lorton, she doesn't care a rap. I don't know how it is, I'm sure," and she held up her needle to thread it, and gave a little sigh of vexation.

Paston, gazing at her as she was thus engaged, felt that his principles were being severely tried by their *tête-à-tête*. He struggled hard, but his opponent's arts were too much for him, and he was forced to give in. Even his voice mutinied: he tried to assume sepulchral gruffness, and only succeeded in emulating with a fidelity that was almost eerie the blatant monotone of a culpably innocent lambkin.

In spite of this mortifying vocal derangement, however, the doctor managed to spend an exceedingly pleasant afternoon, and was in no hurry to change his quarters when Grace hurriedly replaced her work in its basket, exclaiming that they must not delay starting for East Rise another instant, or it would be too late.

Mr. Dalton was roused to accompany them,

and Paston soon found himself chatting pleasantly with Aunt Joan, Miss Hilda having adroitly secured the only other available representative of male humanity, while Grace talked in a low tone to Ursula, who was presiding over the tea-table.

The only person who did not seem quite happy was Mr. Dalton. Confabulations with the excellent Mother Superior always set him seething with irascibility, and on the present occasion he remained in a cantankerous mood for the whole of the ensuing evening. Paston, on the other hand, congratulated himself upon making a friend. He remembered what Grace had said about Robur's enthusiasm for Joanna Blunsden, and felt that he, at any rate, could understand it.

# CHAPTER IV.

## "A GENTLEMAN TO SEE YOU."

"That there is falsehood in his looks
I must and will deny:
They say their master is a knave;
And sure they do not lie."—*Burns.*

THERE must be many happy people in this
much abused world who are not troubled with
any superfluous sense of the eternal fitness of
things. One hears a good deal about "bad
form" and "the correct thing"; but the standard to which those persons refer whose mouths
are full of such suggestions of refinement is nevertheless a low one. It is quite a mistake to suppose that even "society" people are horrified by
incongruity. What incongruities of taste, bearing, dress, language, emotion, will they not gen-
erously tolerate in themselves or their friends?
In the food they eat, in the company they
keep (on alternate occasions), their freedom from
starched or pusillanimous notions of discrimination is indeed remarkable. And if in the matter

of having orthodox opinions,—which is by no means the same thing as acting up to them,—or in the question of family alliances they do hold the reins of their warm, thorough-bred natures just a trifle firmly, are they not obliged by the sacred duty of maintaining appearances to "draw the line somewhere"? In small affairs they are not so rigidly scrupulous. Returning once from a London funeral of more than usual magnificence, the mourning-coaches happened to pass Hyde Park corner. It was the height of the season,—not of funerals, for that goes on all the year round, but of that curious combination of preaching fanaticism and lounging indifference which periodically makes this particular Park a centre of attraction. The chief mourner was a man of secluded and not unthrifty habits: the manners and customs of the new generation were unfamiliar to him, and in the ways of fashion he was quite unversed.

"Why shouldn't we take a ride round among those carriages now we are here?" he asked, to the infinite consternation of his decorously woful fellow-passengers; and he was only hindered by the exercise of muscular persuasion on their part from putting his crape-bedizened visage out of the window, in the absence of a check-string, in order to communicate his wishes to the driver.

It was doubtless from some similar ignorance

or contempt of conventionality that Mr. Lorton did not, as far as can be known, see any valid objection in the fact that it was Sunday against paying his second *visite d'amitié* at East Rise on the day after Paston's unexpected advent, which has been already narrated.

The long-lost father had spent the days since his rebuff in reconsidering with diligent thorough-ness the various circumstances of his friendless and somewhat perilous condition.

To begin with, after brief cogitation, he cursed himself roundly for having accepted defeat at all, and consequently the terms dictated by his opponent. Miss Joanna was a woman, and the thought that he had allowed himself to be van-quished by a member of the opposite sex made his chivalrous nature burn to make effective re-prisals of any form or kind. He was glad of one thing : he had got rid of a certain unlucky trifle in a highly ingenious and advantageous manner. Its possession had kept him constantly on the rack of suspense ; but he no longer had any reason to fear the animosity of its—well, of some-one who had parted with it in rather a queer way ; and on that score at least he could breathe freely.

But though by attentive and assiduous observ-ation he had been enabled to construct and carry out a bold scheme for doing away with a great source of anxiety, no sooner was this gone than another and graver because more certain evil confronted him. His wife had spoken out before her death, and told Joanna Blunsden everything. Oddly enough this contingency never occurred to him till it was realized, and then it so upset his presence of mind that he could see no way out of the difficulty on the spur of the moment but absolute submission.

He had never hated his wife while she was alive as he hated her memory now. What business had she to talk about his private affairs to other people, whatever might be thought of her absconding, he should like to know? It couldn't have mattered a bit to her when she was just going to die; and so she had been mean enough to place him in an extremely awkward position out of pure spite. Too bad! And the worst of it was that this was the last blow in the duel between them, and he had no opportunity of retaliation.

Stop a bit! There was her daughter,—a fitting scape-goat for the sins of the mother, that mother to whom, as she was in her youth, the child presented a strong likeness, though it was scarcely so striking as the surviving parent, with fond infatuation, had induced Joanna to suppose.

The humiliation of defeat was still rankling in this amiable person's bosom when it received

fresh emphasis from the conviction that it had
been incurred quite unnecessarily, and was merely
due to an egregious blunder of his own. Farther
reflection, besides confirming him in this view of
the matter, convinced him that his mistake was
by no means irretrievable. Joanna Blunsden was
not invincible; she had acknowledged as much
to his face; and there was really nothing to prevent him from stealing a march upon her one
vulnerable point, when he would hold the scales
as arbiter of the situation.

The girl—what was her name?—Ursula knew
nothing of his misfortunes and early scrapes;
that was evident, or her protectress would not
have exhibited so much excitement when he
offered to put himself in communication with his
daughter. Her determination had daunted him;
but, after all, the strong-minded old lady's threats
were virtually impotent. Once let him disclose
himself to Ursula, and any attempt to damage
his interests would damage hers to at least an
equal extent. It was the winning card to play:
perhaps it was sheer boyish sentimentality not to
play it at once. Anyhow, he would give his
enemy one more chance: if she refused it, let her
take the consequences. Could he frighten the
girl into obeying him, he would summon her to
accompany him, and share his nomadic life; not
that he was particularly desirous of her com-

panionship for its own sake, but because it would inflict a lifelong sorrow upon " that officious Blunsden woman," as he mentally described Aunt Joan. Even in the event of this ambitious design remaining unconsummated, Ursula would probably feel the shock of meeting her father, and learning his past career, with an emotion more nearly related to terror than to joy. It would pay him to foster that emotion. He would dwell with cynical frankness on all the more repelling details within his experience. To see his child —psha! what meaningless words they were !— to see *her* child shudder and turn faint at his tale was a luxury upon which he must feast his eyes : the Blunsden woman would have to accede to his proposals at a good round figure if he was to forego this treat.

As to finding Ursula when he wanted her, his mind was perfectly easy. During the short armistice he had been on the alert bodily as well as mentally, nor had he prowled about the neighbourhood of the house on East Rise, or attended its occupants at a respectful distance in their walks abroad for nothing. It was a regular little household, and by dint of extreme circumspection, aided by the judicious pumping of a youthful hanger-on or factotum of Miss Blunsden's, whom he waylaid and bribed with half-a-crown, he soon knew all that was necessary for his purpose.

It was a light task for one accustomed to the double-dealing of his fellow-men to manage all this without rousing curiosity. Besides, he was assured that Joanna Blunsden, lulled by a false confidence in the potency of her weapons, would not wake to the necessity of removing her charge out of harm's reach till all such precautions should be fruitless. A similar mine would be laid under the daughter's feet to that which had threatened to explode beneath the father for more than half his life, and all who loved her would be careful to avert the catastrophe which must befall her concomitantly with his destruction. Thus he might confidently expect not only to have the satisfaction of snapping his fingers at Miss Joanna, but also to see that lady actually forced into active co-operation with Ursula to screen him from the tardy approach of justice.

He was fully equipped, therefore, to reopen the campaign when he made his second attack upon the citadel that Sunday afternoon.

Before effecting an entrance, however, he scanned the house-front with the practised self-possession of one who was on terms of intimacy with its internal arrangements. Glancing at Miss Hilda's bedroom window, he was gratified to observe that the blind was drawn down, thereby signifying that the fair tenant of the chamber was disposed neither to interrupt nor be interrupted for the next hour and a half at least, that being rather less than the time which must elapse before tea would be sent up to the drawing-room, unless something should occur to throw the household economy out of gear. The window just above —that of Ursula's sitting-room—was shut, and Lorton knew that the girl generally threw it open when she went out. Probably she was up there now; at any rate he was sure that Miss Joanna would find means of keeping her there out of the way so long as her father remained in the house.

The next step was final; his boldness was spiced with insolent exultation as he took it. Enquiring for his unconscious foe by her full name this time, he was admitted after a short parley. By the singular luck which always seemed to befriend him, he found her alone. His calculation about Ursula had been correct, then.

Joanna was startled; she betrayed more alarm at his appearance now than when he had first announced his identity to her. But if her emotions were strong her will was no weak one. By the time that she had turned round in her chair so as to face her visitor without rising her mastery over herself was completely regained.

"If anyone else calls I don't want to be

disturbed while this —— while we are still engaged here together," she said to the discreet handmaid, as Lorton sat down composedly, and they were left to themselves. It may have been an old maid's prejudice, but she could not degrade the title of gentleman by applying it to him before a servant, who might understand it literally.

" Now, sir, no doubt you had a good reason for breaking the terms of our compact without consulting me in writing; have the goodness to lose no time in acquainting me with it."

She took off her spectacles, put them into their case, and sat drumming it softly against her knuckles, looking very watchfully on the defensive.

" The fact is, Miss Blunsden, I am discontented with your terms," he began with suave deliberation. " I must confess I was not attracted when you originally proposed them—with some assumption of authority, if you remember. Ah, well," he continued, accepting the meaning conveyed in her gesture of impatience, " those conditions have not grown any lighter to my mind during the interval in which I have been trying to get used to them. Indeed, they seem so much more onerous than I had anticipated that really I cannot rest satisfied with them at all, and I must beg you, my dear madam, to reconsider your harsh—unintentionally so, no doubt, but still somewhat harsh—decision."

In spite of the servility of his words, the tone in which he preferred his request betrayed a triumphant certainty that it would be granted. His hearer's heart failed her as she listened.

" You think you have discovered some means of forcing me," she said incredulously.

The remark carried balm to her enemy's soul. " She gives splendid sport," he thought to himself ; " why, to look at her you would think she was more impregnable than ever ! "

" Not at all," he sighed, and affected perplexity. Then he added, " What makes you think that ? "

" I had occasion when I last spoke with you to tell you not to fence with me," observed Joanna, answering him but not his question ; "perhaps you will have the goodness not to do so now."

" It's hard to be forced to contradict a lady," said the other, simulating a mien of grovelling dejection, " but I trust you will see the injustice of your suspicion of me, Miss Blunsden, when I say that I present myself here before you this Sabbath afternoon solely to claim your compassion for my childless and friendless state."

Another bad shot on his part. It was the absent sister, the slumbering Hilda, whose chair he was even now polluting with his godless coat-tails, who wore her religion upon her sleeve.

Joanna's reply pained him by its lack of sympathy.

"You have doubtless been to church once to-day, Mr. Lorton;" here she looked at her watch; "perhaps you might like to go again; you will be just in time for afternoon service at the parish church if you bestir yourself. At any rate, I have no wish to detain you," she added with cruel coldness.

"I regret to say that I cannot leave you without an answer. Won't you think better of your refusal to do something for me?"

His audacity in again returning to the demand for hush-money, after it had been so successfully resisted, astounded her to a degree which made it impossible for her to articulate a reply.

"Because, if you don't see your way to doing so," he went on,—and there was a malignant nonchalance in his manner which would have provoked any one strong enough for the purpose to throw him out of the window without taking the trouble to open it first,—"if you can't provide me, in short, with a small but sufficient sum of money down, pledging yourself to renew the same at future periods to be agreed on between ourselves, I fear the terms of our contract will

shortly be broken rather more seriously than they
have been by my coming here to-day."

He paused to observe the effect of his words
upon Joanna. It was somewhat disappointing
to an eager, susceptible nature like his. Viewed
as a dramatic effort, his performance so far had
fallen extremely flat.

" Plague take the woman, she doesn't know
when she's beaten ; but I'll punish her." His
soliloquy was cut short by the object of his silent
malediction.

" I recommend you not to try me any more
with your changes of mind, Mr. Lorton," said she
sternly. " When I offer you peace once more,
and for the last time, on the old terms, you know
well enough that I am as lenient towards you as
it is possible for me to be. That is my ultimatum ; neglect it at your own risk. If you agree
to it you must never let me see you or hear of
you again. Leave Burnport within a week, or I
will have you watched."

Joanna's voice was as calm as it had been all
through the interview ; but her visitor could
guess from her quickened breathing how effectually he had fanned her resentment against him
into a flame.

" Dear me, that is extremely unfortunate," he
rejoined, showing his teeth in an ill-favoured
smile, " because I had hoped you would see things

in a different light after your first very natural
and candid expression of annoyance at finding I
was alive and, if not kicking, at any rate robust.
But has it ever struck you," he proceeded,
suddenly changing his manner to something
more aggressive, "did it never occur to you, my
excellent Miss Blunsden, that I might refuse
your ultimatum, as you call it, very much at
someone else's risk as well as at my own?"

Joanna's hands were trembling. "What do
you mean?" was all she could say.

"Merely this, that if you put Scotland Yard
on my track, the blow you aim at me will
descend upon the girl too, as surely as though
she were standing in my shoes. Your ultimatum has recoiled upon your own head, it
seems. I gave you your chance, and you refused
it. Very well; within the next twenty-four
hours your precious darling shall know all about
me; I have made up my mind, and you are
powerless to prevent it."

Never was transition more complete: had the
evidence of his innate brutality been stamped
upon his brow, the revelation could not have
been more unmistakable than his words and
bearing made it.

"Now," said the bereaved parent with ironical
emphasis, at the same time making a feint of
picking his hat off the floor where he had placed

it, "there being nothing further to say, I suppose it's not necessary for me to do violence to my feelings as a man of honour by staying any longer in a lady's house in defiance of her wishes."

"Stay." Joanna motioned him to wait till she could collect herself sufficiently to discuss the question in the light of this new departure. The mere novelty of the situation stunned her; the creature whom a moment ago she was spurning under her feet was now actually placing the yoke upon her own neck in the coolest way imaginable.

Presently, without heeding his taunts, she spoke :

"What must I do?"

The hollowness of her voice proclaimed her entire capitulation. Her victor swelled with pride at having so skilfully crushed all the resistance out of her. She was prepared to sacrifice even principle for the girl's sake, then. He chuckled under his breath.

"I must say, Miss Blunsden, you expect a good deal of me if you think I am going to re-open the whole of this painful negotiation."

He found her suspense so extremely entertaining that it was difficult to resist any opportunity of prolonging it.

As she remained silent, however, and gave no further sign of agitation, except what was conveyed in her bent head and clasped hands, he proceeded to observe, with a short laugh,—

"Make it worth my while, and I'll never trouble you any more."

"Well," rejoined his fallen foe, raising her head and regarding him steadfastly, "give me time—a week,—and I will tell you the outside sum which I can part with as the price of your daughter's happiness."

Perhaps she was as unconscious as he of the sting conveyed in those last words; but her composure simply baffled him. However did she manage to rally in this marvellous manner?

Nothing could be lost by accepting her proposal, however; so he resolved to accede gracefully to it, and stay all proceedings for the present, or at least so to pretend, which would do just as well.

"Look here, Miss Blunsden, I'll return good for evil," he remarked in a tone that struggled hard to sound relenting, but only succeeded in being slightly less rasping than before.

"What did you offer to do for me? Nothing —till you were obliged. Even now you're suspicious of me. But I'll not be suspicious of you; I'll allow you what you've asked for, and you needn't expect me again till this day week. Mind you're ready with your answer then.

Should our little business fall through after all, you know what to expect. Good afternoon, my dear madam. Pray don't exert yourself to ring; I'd rather go unseen, if you've no objection. No? really very obliging of you."

After he had gone Joanna sat with her elbows on the little table in front of her, resting her head on her hands, while her eyes gazed vacantly at the wall opposite. She had succumbed; there was no help for it. A less scrupulous person in her position might have seized the time still at command to put the police on Lorton's track. If he were arrested within a week he would be prevented from communicating with Ursula for the next fifteen years or so. But then, supposing he outlived his term of penal servitude, an extremely probable contingency too—. No; even had the doctrine that all is fair in war been acceptable to Joanna, it would simply be a cowardly postponement of the difficulty to apply it in the present case. Supposing her to be capable of breaking faith with any one, perfidious or not, was she to defer the blow which must fall sooner or later, and which, if it fell later, would in all likelihood spend its accumulated force on the girl's head alone? The child must not be exposed to braving this danger by herself: she should have at least one poor, weak friend to bear it with her.

"If only there was someone to talk to about it," replied the poor woman; "but Hilda is no good, and Arnold has gone off no one knows where; it's a dreadful thing to carry all this responsibility on a single pair of shoulders.— Well, Mary, what is it?" She broke off her meditations as the door opened.

"If you please, ma'am, there's a gentleman down-stairs as would like to see you, and I told him I thought you was engaged, but would he wait a minute while I came and asked you, and he said he would, so——"

"What, another gentleman!" exclaimed Mary's mistress.

"Yes, ma'am; Mr. Paston, ma'am; he said—"

"There, show him up," said Miss Joanna, checking her maid's volubility; and forthwith up the doctor was shown.

He could not avoid giving a slight start as he shook hands with her, and observed the ashy hue of her face, and its contracted appearance, so different from the look which it had worn on the previous day.

That look began, however, to return to some extent while they talked, he starting with an apology about calling again so soon.

"But, indeed, I have only come just to say good-bye," he concluded. "I dare say you have had someone to entertain before me, so I will not tire you further. Pray remember me to Miss Blunsden and your niece, and let me look forward to seeing you again when I next come to Burnport, or you go to London."

"Please don't go, Mr. Paston; your visit does not tire me, it is a godsend."

Thus adjured, Paston placed a chair on the other side of Joanna's table, and sat down without a word.

"You may have seen someone — a man — leave the house as you came in," she went on. "He has only just left me; once before he came, and each time he has brought me dreadful news."

"Ah!" ejaculated the doctor, in a manner which suggested that he had all along suspected as much, and that he could even make a shrewd · guess at the nature of the news, if he was put to it. After all, the use of this professional monosyllable had become so habitual to him that any person of average discernment would have seen it at once to be purely involuntary, a mere illustration of reflex action, like the "If you please, will you tell me the time?" with which town-bred youngsters never fail to victimize the proud possessor of a watch.

"I saw your friend, I think," said the doctor, before Joanna could resume; "but not outside. He was down below, in your dining-room, when I came up. However, he may have gone now;

I heard the front door shut almost immediately after I came up-stairs."

His companion gave a suppressed cry of alarm. "Excuse me for a moment," she said; "I must go and see if he is still there," and she hurriedly left the room.

Paston did not follow her. He wondered to see her so distraught.

"It must be something pretty bad to affect a strong woman like her so much," he pondered.

In a minute or two Joanna returned, looking intensely relieved.

"He has gone," she said. "Forgive me; I hardly know what I am doing; I have no one to turn to. Mr. Paston, let me explain; it is too much for me to bear alone."

Hurriedly and disjointedly she poured out the whole story, while Paston listened in silence. "And now," she ended, "there is only a week, one week, for my darling—and I can do nothing —nothing."

"I suppose I am to understand that you have told me all this under the seal of confession, as it were, and merely in the hope that I may be able to suggest some honourable course which has not already occurred to you?"

He spoke slowly and feelingly: any attempt to describe his sympathy for her would have seemed almost sacrilegious. Inadequate words

do no good; they only jar upon the mind.
Where the woe is real and pressing sympathy
has no time to invent phrases, and best expresses
itself indirectly.

"Yes," and Joanna looked up again; "you
must keep my secret safe, and not turn the
information I have given you against him. I
should not shrink from giving him up to justice
myself, if it were the only way. But I have
promised, and it is neither possible to place
Ursula beyond his reach without telling her
why, or to have him shut up before he can get
at her."

Paston hesitating, she continued self-reproach-
fully,—

"It was thoughtless of me to burden you
hastily with this upon so slight an acquaintance.
I ought not to have done so; but I am in such
straits, and some instinct—I couldn't help it—
guided me."

There was a tendency in her voice to become
wild; but she quelled it with an effort.

"You were Arnold Robur's greatest friend,—
he has often spoken of you to me in this very
room,—so your name was familiar to me, and I
thought I might confide in you as I should have
done in him if he had been here, and come in
opportunely, as you did. We seemed to understand each other yesterday so well, too; and

when you came in to-day I welcomed you quite as I would welcome an old friend. It is hard to impose the duties of friendship upon you at such an early stage ; I am afraid you must be thinking very ill of me for doing so."

"Miss Blunsden," said the doctor gravely, "I am troubled, it is true, but not about trifles of etiquette. What you have just said, however, emboldens me to ask you a favour. You say you would tell Robur if he were in my place ; will you let me tell him, on the same condition of secrecy, if I see him before you do ? He would be your natural confidant, and there is nothing to be risked by letting him share our knowledge."

"Yes," assented Joanna simply ; "I trust you both implicitly."

"Very well," returned Paston, shaking himself as though he felt satisfied at having settled that point ; "now let us look this thing in the face."

   *     *     *     *     *

Meanwhile, what was the guileless object of these machinations about ? He had parted from his audacious opponent with such an elegant display of courtesy as was a fitting termination to their encounter. He was descending the stairs with dignity, musing upon the gallantry with which he had carried all before him, while a pardonable exhilaration at his victory warmed him just comfortably, when there came

the sound of a step outside the front door, followed by a decided jerk of the bell-handle. He
quickened his pace in order that he might take
refuge in the dining-room from the observation
of strangers on either side of the door. The room
was empty, and in he slid just in time. A
moment later there were voices outside, and
then, before he could conceal himself, a man
stepped in from the hall.

"If you'll wait there, sir, I'll see whether Miss
Joanna is disengaged," said the maid from outside, as she departed on her errand.

The pair in the dining-room faced each other
for little more than a second. Lorton turned his
back and walked to the window. Paston opened
his lips sufficiently to emit a very soft, almost
inaudible whistle, but did not stir from the
door-way.

"Will you step this way, please, sir."

It was the maid; she only came half-way
down, seeing him standing there, and he turned
round to follow her at once.

"Can't be mistaken," he muttered; "he's a
good deal altered about the lower part of his
face,—used to wear a thumping beard,—but I
should have known the fellow anywhere."

"The fellow" remained by the window in a
state of manifest perturbation. This accidental
recognition by an old acquaintance seemed to

agitate him.   He went out into the hall, opened
the front door, and shut it to again sharply.
Then he listened.  Nothing happened.  He went
back into the dining-room and deliberated with
himself.  The doctor knew him, he was certain
of it ; and the doctor would tell his friends,
especially one friend, a friend whose existence
had been troublesome to Mr. Lorton, and might
under some circumstances become so again.
Truly the combination against him was more
formidable than he had supposed.  The facts of
the case were altered since he made his compact
with the Blunsden woman a few minutes ago.
Did not the said alteration exonerate him from
observing it ?  Why should he hesitate any longer
to take the step which was to secure his future
prosperity, whether they liked it or not?  He
would take that step.  If they chose to combine
against him on the sly, that was their look-out ;
let them abide by the results of their perfidy.

He took off his shoes, and stole with them in
his hand cautiously out into the hall once more.
No one was about, and the door at the top of
the kitchen stairs was closed.

He crept stealthily up-stairs.

# CHAPTER V.

## "HONOUR THY FATHER."

"I? what I answered? as I live,
I never fancied such a thing
As answer possible to give.
What says the body when they spring
Some monstrous torture-engine's whole
Strength on it? No more says the soul."

*R. Browning.*

LORTON had only just reached the landing above the drawing-room when he was struck with sudden alarm, for the door beneath opened, and a hurried step passed down the stair. He stood like a stone, making no sound, and breathed freely again only when he heard Joanna return to her visitor. "Gad, what a shave!" he thought; "that confounded woman would have spoilt the whole game if she'd caught me in the house again with the doctor about. She's infernally suspicious." The victim of unkind thoughts sighed to himself at the cold, calculating prudence of a world too harsh for such guileless natures as his. Then he turned his attention to business. Now that he was safe he might as well make sure what he was going to do. If Ursula was like her mother, he was likely to have an interesting little scene.

He ascended to the next floor, where Ursula's sitting-room was, and took his bearings. The window looked out on the street, so there could be no doubt as to the door. An unwonted feeling of nervousness came over him—he might find the business on hand a trifle ticklish. Never mind; it was well worth the risk, if it was only for the score off his enemy down-stairs. No; he wouldn't put on his boots. Doubtless it would be better for some purposes, but this particular pair were unluckily creaky, and Paston was downstairs; it wouldn't do. " It's about as well that other chap's eyes weren't as good as the doctor's, blame him : the whole thing would have been settled up long ago most uncomfortably. The persistent way in which people badger a poor devil is positively brutal," thought Mr. Lorton.

He went up to the door. Knock ? Politer, no doubt, but not so effective. Surely a father might come into his own daughter's boudoir (pretty word, boudoir) without these extravagant ceremonies. No, he wouldn't knock. He turned the handle and opened the door.

Ursula was standing by the window, looking

out over the grey, foam-flecked sea, whose sullen
murmur was distinctly audible.  She turned
round in some surprise as the door opened, for
she had heard no step outside.  " Well, aunt,"
she began with a smile—then she stopped suddenly, startled and alarmed.  Who was this ? She
knew the face well enough, but what business
had he here ?  The blood rushed to her face as
she made a half-unconscious movement towards
the bell, and then paused again.

Lorton was gratified; his dramatic instincts
found considerable food for enjoyment in the
situation.  " A deuced pretty bit of flesh," he
thought: " promises sport."  His teeth showed
again in the same malignant smile.

" Miss Lorton, I believe ? " he said with an air
of exaggerated politeness.

Ursula was both puzzled and alarmed, for she
had no clue whatever as to the meaning of this
man's presence.  But she had no lack of courage.

" I am Miss Lorton," she replied ; " but I am
not accustomed to receiving visitors here."  She
faced him boldly, but her voice trembled in spite
of her.

" Very proper, very proper indeed ; I shouldn't
allow it myself," and he closed the door calmly.

" I said that I do not receive visitors here.
What right have you to come ?  Leave the room,
or I shall ring the bell."

"Oh no; pardon me, but that is one thing I cannot possibly allow. It goes to my heart to deny a pretty girl anything, you know, but ringing the bell and leaving the room are just two things that are at present quite out of the question. Really, this is a very delightful little room;" and Lorton glanced round it with the air of a connoisseur.

Ursula was helpless : a rapid movement on the stranger's part had enabled him effectually to cover the way either to the bell or the door. Some girls might have screamed, and possibly that would have been the best course under the circumstances. But it was some fifteen years since Ursula had tried it, and it did not occur to her as the thing to do now. So she stood silent, with her hand on the back of a chair, watching.

The other was in no hurry. Paternal fondness was not one of his prominent characteristics. Of course Ursula was his child; but that only affected him from the pecuniary point of view. He regarded her as a valuable piece of goods just discovered, for whom her protectress might give him money down, and who, failing that, would be a useful addition to his household. There was no doubt that he would make her pay. But as for sparing her because she was his daughter, that would be contemptible weakness

to which no sane man would ever descend. And
pity was the last thing her beauty suggested to
him ; on the contrary, it greatly heightened the
enjoyment of the position. Lorton was a man of
pretty taste ; when he had got hold of a victim,
the lovelier she was the better. The pious souls
of the Roman populace under the emperors, or
the spectators of an *auto-da-fé* in the days of the
Inquisition, were never quite satisfied by withered
matrons or bearded blasphemers : it was the young
and lovely virgins whom they really enjoyed seeing in the arena or at the stake. Lorton was
thoroughly in sympathy with these worthies, and
had no intention of unnecessarily shortening the
little drama. Even if the " Blunsden woman's "
sufferings in prospect had not stirred him, he
would have felt that an hour spent here would
be well repaid.

"Your own drawings ? " he enquired blandly.
" H'm. Deficient perhaps in maturity of handling, but promising. You will doubtless improve. Literature—doesn't seem altogether becoming to a young lady. Dante—Goethe—a
German scholar ! that is charming ; a most
useful language, but not a patch on French.
Learned doubtless from the Blunsden—what's
her name—Joanna." Ursula quivered : Lorton
smiled again. " Well," he went on, " haven't you
anything to say ? " She was silent. " Temper.

Ah! a sad thing; so troublesome. My dear, you must learn to curb your angry passions."

"This is too much!" exclaimed Ursula: "let me go. How dare you speak to me in this manner?" She tried to pass him, but he caught her by the wrist.

"Gently, gently. Excitement brings a charming colour to your cheeks; and your eyes—by Jove, they're splendid. But it's bad for you; brings on palpitation, you know."

"Who are you?" said Ursula panting, her eyes blazing with wrath. He looked at her with admiration as she faced him.

"First-rate: we'll have you on the stage yet. Never thought of that before;" and he scanned her with a critical leer.

"Who are you?" she said again, her breast heaving.

"Business-like too—another excellent quality, not, I regret to say, derived from your mother. Your useful traits are developing charmingly. Who am I?"—he let go of her wrist—"my dear Ursula, I am your long-absent but fond papa."

Did you ever receive suddenly and unexpectedly a blinding blow between the eyes? That is something like the feeling which Ursula now experienced. She turned dizzy, and only saved herself from falling to the floor by catching hold of a chair, and so dropped on to a sofa, her eyes

fixed for the first time in real terror on her tor-
mentor. The mockery in his words was lost on
her—the blow was too tremendous. She trembled
in every limb.

Lorton paused. Not that any thought of
mercy entered into him; but he had hardly
counted on the full effect of his words, and for
a moment he was almost frightened by her pallor.
So he held his peace to give her time to recover.
She was a stout-hearted girl, however, and soon
rallied; the look of terror gave place to one of
suffering endurance. The father found a deep
satisfaction in his daughter's pluck; besides, he
had not half done with her. He had no mind
to miss a single torture which might be inflicted
with tolerable safety. He was an epicure who
liked to try the flavour of every dish.

"Well," he said, "this is gratifying. I always
expected my return to be hailed with passionate
outpourings of delight; but I don't think I ever
reckoned on such a display of emotion as this.
But you haven't said how glad you are to see me
yet." He could see how she was suffering and he
felt an infernal delight in her pain. Poor girl,
she was perfectly helpless before him. She never
dreamed of doubting the truth of his words;
how could she resist him?

"I fear," he went on, letting his hard eyes
rest on her face with an enjoyment partly

æsthetic, partly bloodthirsty, "you are scarcely
the sort of girl that it gives a yearning parent
complete satisfaction to find. The prodigal son,
if I remember rightly, was received with open
arms and a good dinner by his affectionate
father; but the returning father is not, as far as
I can see, going to be greeted with fatted calves,
to say nothing of embraces." He seated himself
coolly beside her, but she shrank from him.

"By the Lord," he said emphatically, "you
*are* a handsome girl," and he ratified his criticism
with another oath. "You *shall* go on the stage ;
you'd make a fortune there. With that face and
figure you would be the rage in a week. There
wouldn't be a dry eye in the house if you acted
on the boards as you're doing now. That look
you gave me just now would carry the newspapers
by storm, and we'd give you an extra special
puff all to yourself in the *Tuba*. We will, by
Jupiter !" The man was appraising the poor girl's
market value as if she had been a bale of indigo.

"Well, what have you to say to me now ? "

"I have nothing to say," answered Ursula in
a low voice that sounded in her own ears as if
it belonged to someone else. "I have nothing
to say." She did not move. Her hands were
clasped together—Lorton could see how tightly.

"What! you aren't going to welcome your
dad ? "

Ursula's only answer was a look—a look of appealing agony, which would have gone to the heart of any less hardened blackguard than her own father; but he was delighted by it.

"Ophelia, by Jove! No, Desdemona would be better still: and, by gad, I'll try the part of Iago myself. I always had a hankering to see what I could do with Iago. Well, that remains for the future. Meantime, what do you suppose you are going to do?"

"Father," she said—"you say you are my father; have some pity on me, and leave me—leave me to myself." Her voice broke so that the last words were barely audible.

Lorton rose. There was no fear of her trying to escape him. The bird was in the snare now; she might beat her wings as she liked, but she was fast. He walked to the window and looked out. There were few people in the streets; church not over yet. There was plenty of time.

He turned towards Ursula. She had not moved, except that she had turned her face with its pleading eyes to watch him.

"Come," he said, "a cat may look at a king, but that's no reason why you should keep staring at me. I guess you'll recognize your father next time he has the honour of meeting you. That's just the way of glaring at a fellow your mother used to have." The man actually spoke as if he was deeply aggrieved by the unjustifiable conduct of those who were nearest to him—and should have been dearest.

Ursula tried to turn her eyes aside but could not, the fascination was too strong. At the mention of her mother she trembled, and grew even whiter than she was before.

"Frightened, are you? No doubt; you have no one to help you now that young fool Robur's gone."

If she was white before she became crimson now. The hot blood surged up at Arnold's name till neck and cheek and brow were all aglow. Convulsively she tightened the clasp of her hands, and a low moan broke from her.

He paused to extract full and exquisite enjoyment from the spectacle. He felt that he was paying off vast arrears of debt to his dead wife in the person of the daughter who was so like her. Racks and stakes and thumbscrews belonged to a merely barbarous age; folks who believed in them knew nothing of scientific torture: they had no delicacy or refinement. But then it is no doubt true that few persons are so favoured by fortune as to find a victim as perfect as Ursula.

"You get more like your mother every moment," he went on; "and I've a notion you have her temper too. Most handsome girls have

a devil in them, I've noticed; and the worst I
ever knew was Mary."

Ursula was roused again. Lorton was not
always a successful diplomatist : the other day
he had suffered a crushing defeat at Joanna
Blunsden's hands; but in the devices of downright cruelty he was an adept. Besides, he had
his experience of his own wife's character to
guide him now; and it would never do simply
to crush the girl. The victims of the " punishment jacket" in Charles Reade's novel were
periodically revived by a pailful of cold water;
Lorton's method was more artistic, and it was
no less successful.

She spoke again, and her voice had become
hard and stern ; the pleading tone had gone out
of it.

" You have not spared me, and I have borne
your cruel words. But I will not bear to hear
you abuse my mother. You know how you
treated her when she lived: beware how you
slander her in her grave."

" Very pretty and melodramatic ; but even
my consideration for my daughter's feelings will
not justify me in falsifying the facts, you know.
That would be immoral. Of course I should
like to be able to tell you that your dear mother
was the angel you doubtless fancy her; but I
greatly regret that I feel bound to say she had

a devil of a temper. Now don't say you won't
bear it,"—Ursula opened her lips to speak,—
"because you can't help yourself. You've got
to bear it, whether you like it or not. It is
becoming in you to doubt the assertion, but you
don't seem troubled with scruples as to believing
all you hear about your father."

Seeing that she made no attempt to answer
he went on, after seating himself in a chair
opposite her, close to the fire.

"You don't seem interested in your loving
father now that you have found him again—or
perhaps I should say now that he has found you.
You evince no passionate yearning to learn how
he has spent the last twenty years or so. Apparently it makes no difference to you whether he
has been passing the time in wealth and comfort,
or poverty with cold mutton for dinner. But I
think it would be good for you to hear a little
about it; and in fact I don't mind going back
earlier.

"There was a little accident some three-and-
twenty years ago—we needn't go into details—
which made me think that a change of air would
suit my constitution, and I left my native heath,
not without some small lingering regrets. By a
singular coincidence, another little accident only
a few months later induced your mother to try
a change of air too; and strangely enough, she

selected the same salubrious climate I had chosen.
A farther remarkable chain of events resulted in
our meeting; and as a gentleman of refined
education was almost as great a rarity out there
as a lady whose only qualifications for society
were a handsome face and a tolerable acquaintance with literature on the top of the ordinary
accomplishments, we naturally foregathered, and
entered into a contract for our mutual convenience. Of course we talked a lot about love and
that sort of trash; but that is about as genuine
in the antipodes' as it is in England. Would
you believe," said Mr. Lorton, stirring the fire
meditatively, " would you believe that she actually
tried to carry on the same nonsense after we
were spliced? I pointed out to her that marriage
was simply a business transaction; a handsome
girl is a very useful partner in some professions,
and if I kept her from starving, which she would
infallibly have done but for me, hang it, she
ought to have been grateful. She objected to
my companions; she objected to swearing; she
objected to assisting in the intoxication of my
friends. By the Lord! I never saw such a d—d
cantankerous woman." He looked maliciously
towards Ursula to see how she took this hit;
but her lips only tightened a little. " Game, by
Jove!" he thought; "never had such sport in
my life. The Blunsden is too old and tough

for the real thing; but, by gad, the girl's splendid."

"Excuse me ; but you know these reminiscences are highly interesting to me, and ought to be so to you, because I fancy you appeared on the scenes pretty soon after. And, upon my soul, you didn't improve matters. There's a devil in most babies that sets them howling and squalling when they're not wanted, and I should think there never was a devil so cursedly noisy as yours. Changed his ways now, and don't seem to set you screaming like some others, but I guess he's there still. Got sulky, I suppose. Well, as I was saying, you didn't improve matters. You squalled, and the wife seemed to forget that she had a husband to look after, to love and to cherish, as the prayer-book says,—oh, I haven't forgotten that, I assure you,—to say nothing of obeying." (It seems to have escaped Mr. Lorton's memory that the husband also undertakes to love and to cherish his wife ; the reciprocal character of the transaction was not a subject on which he suffered his mind to dwell with any force.) "And what was worse, as if a squalling kid wasn't enough, she took to crying herself. I might as well have married the Trafalgar Square fountain—better, because that generally doesn't work. Well, I did my little best to improve her. Such powers of persuasion

as Providence thought fit to bestow on me I
exerted on her. I exhausted my vocabulary for
her benefit on an average, I should say, three
times a day. But she only got worse, and at
last she hooked it. Sweet wifelike conduct to
desert one's husband, I call it. And now, by
Jove, what did she do by way of compensation?
Gave her daughter her own cursed temper, and
taught her to hate her father seemingly," and
Mr. Lorton's countenance assumed an expression
of disgust at the wicked ways of woman.

Pale and dry-eyed, Ursula sat and heard him.
Do what she would, she winced terribly under
his words, and now and then she could not but
show it. The soul of the affectionate husband
and parent thrilled with a keen delight as he
saw his victim quiver beneath his merciless
stabs.

" Perhaps you feel a trifle less proud of your
mother now ;—by the way, you may learn from
my veracious narrative to curb your angry
passions, and behave a little better than she did.
But you shall feel prouder of your father before
you've done. You would like to hear how I've
prospered since? A deal better than before, I
assure you. I thought I had got a help-meet,
and I found I had got nothing but a clog, two
clogs when you were born ; and, by Jove, I was
thankful to be rid of you both. As for my way

of getting my living, that's neither here nor there. I've tried a good lot in my time, from thimble-rigging and billiard-marking to news-paper work. Gambling is good, because if the cards don't come right of themselves a skilful player can make them. But that's risky. I was caught once, and if I hadn't shot the other chap first and sworn *he* was cheating — that happened in Texas—I guess I should have been off the hooks by now. But I left Texas. There are too many flies there. Oh, I've kept myself pretty comfortable; you needn't be troubled on that score. But you see I want to be comfort-able at the expense of less exertion. I want some peace and quietness, and I want some money. But we haven't come to that stage yet; I want you to hear a trifle more first.

" I came back to England after that little affair in Texas, and I've tried round a good many professions. Perhaps the most uncomfort-able experience I ever had was at Epsom. It's not a pleasant sensation to hear a weltering mob yelling ' Welcher,' and I really think I had a closer scrape that time than even in Texas; but I got off. Then I got on the *Tuba* business, and that certainly has its merits. Diplomatic finesse was always my strong point, and it has free play there. There is something so thoroughly satis-factory about turning a man round one's little finger, or, better still, getting him under your thumb, and letting him know that your thumb is only waiting till his use is over to flatten him ; it is really a delicious sensation : I do enjoy seeing a man squirm. But dear me, how I digress ! " (Lorton considered he was safe so long as Joanna was engaged with the doctor.) " That isn't at all what I meant to say. I was down at Brighton a few weeks ago, and circumstances made it convenient for me to visit a certain churchyard there. I was not, I own, wildly surprised to see your mother's gravestone there—a temper like hers would wear any one out before long."

Ursula's eyes flashed again, roused by the utter heartlessness of his words.

" There now, take care, or you'll be following her example, and the English stage will lose the charming young lady who is destined to be its brightest ornament. As I was going to say, that was the first news I had of your mother's death. I don't know that I dropped a tear on the grave ; but the knowledge simplified matters a bit. Well then, other circumstances brought me here—business in connection with a young gentleman who didn't know me, but who does know you. When I saw him walking with a girl I was interested ; but, by Jupiter, when I saw the girl's face I was—well, you might have knocked me down with a feather. I should hardly have known you from your mother a little before I married her. So I knew you must be my long-lost and yearned-for child; and of course, when I heard that your name was Ursula Lorton, why that settled the question.

"And now we come to something I was talking about just now. Having found you—well, I don't mean my discovery to go for nothing. I want money; do you understand? Money."

He leaned back in his chair and looked at Ursula, expecting a response.

"Why do you say this to me?" she answered wearily, with a hopeless ring in her voice; "why have you come here to tell me this? You want money, you say; but I have none."

"True, my child. You at present have none, being up to the present time merely the recipient of Miss Blunsden's bounty—no better than a charity girl. But then, I must have money, and you must see that I get it."

"What do you mean? How can I get you money?"

"My good girl, that is a question that shouldn't puzzle a babe. How are you to get it? Don't you know the Blunsden woman down-stairs would do anything for you?"

Lorton knew how to torture his daughter; but he had not the dimmest conception of how to manage her. He fancied that she was utterly crushed, and he could do what he liked with her. To his regret and surprise, he found this impression entirely mistaken. Instead of unresisting acquiescence, he was met by an outburst of indignation.

"Do you dare to ask me to go to Miss Blunsden and beg? to show my gratitude for all her goodness and kindness to me and my mother— the mother who met with little enough kindness from you—by robbing her of her little store to keep you at your ease? I will not." Ursula had risen, and stood face to face with her parent, her eyes flashing, her whole form quivering with indignation. The scorn in her voice was scathing.

Lorton was taken aback. His experience had not taught him to understand what a true woman may bear. The girl had allowed him to set before her the revolting picture of his own life, to brand the sense of his infamy, her father's infamy, upon her heart. She had listened and endured this suffering as only a woman would, with scarcely a word, without a tear. And he thought she was crushed therefore! Had the pain indeed been less terrible, she might no doubt have found relief in tears, and he was right in taking her silence as the strongest proof of her anguish; but he was hopelessly astray if he thought Ursula's spirit might be so broken.

He did not know what to make of this reception
of his proposal. He resolved to try bullying.

"Come, drop that," he said. "Don't try to
come over me with your tragedy airs. They're
very fine and high-sounding, and very pretty on
paper or on the boards; but they won't do here.
Do as I tell you, or it will be the worse for you."

But Ursula was not to be brow-beaten. She
had forgotten her pain in her indignation.

"You cannot frighten me," she said; "you
might have seen that by now. As for doing
what you tell me, I answer again, I will not. I
will not ask Miss Blunsden for one penny."

"H'm. Well, perhaps it'll be better. I don't
know that the Blunsdens have enough. But, by
gad, I know who has. You shall marry young
Robur, and I'll come and tell him afterwards.
And, by the Lord, I'll have my money, and my
revenge on you both."

The girl gasped for breath; for a moment she
thought she should faint; it was too horribly
cruel. Suddenly she sank on to the sofa and
burst into a passion of sobs.

"So I've broken you at last, have I? I
thought it wouldn't go on much longer." He
paused and watched her for a little, then went
on again with cold, merciless deliberation. "You
have tried to resist me, but you're beaten. I
didn't think of that plan before, but it shall be

done. I know how you feel about each other ; I
can have him at your feet again in a moment.
You will marry him ; and then when I come to
him, and tell him who is his wife's father, and
what his wife's father has done, I guess there
won't be much difficulty about hush-money.
And then, by G—, you shall see what comes
of your attempts to defy me, when he turns from
a forger's child with hatred. I see it all, and I
swear I never before dreamed of revenge such as
I shall get now."

"Oh no, no!" moaned Ursula through her
tears. " I would die rather than do that. Father!
father! have you no mercy ?"

"Mercy? Do you think I'm a girl like yourself? Do you think I am going to spare you
because I have made you cry at last ? Not I.
You are going to do what I tell you—I'm too
old a bird to be taken in by the water-works
trick."

" Do what you like ; I am helpless—helpless
—you know that. But I will die rather than do
what you bid me."

The violence of her passion was over now,
but the nervous strain had been too much for her
to bear; and the suddenness of the last blow
had broken her down. She still sobbed, but
quietly now.

Again Lorton was taken aback by the resolution

that sounded in her voice despite its tremulous-
ness.

"She means it, by Jove," he thought. "But
I'll beat her yet. Not now—it'll take time.
She's the stubbornest hussy that ever I met."

"You won't do it? Well then, I'll give you
an alternative. Either what I have said, or come
home with me; I'll see that you pay your keep,
and a good bit over. Come; d' you think you're
going through life without doing a thing for your
father?"

"Home—with you?"

"Yes; home with me. Don't you like the
prospect? D' you think I'm going to let you run
to waste? How d' you expect to support yourself? The Blunsden woman won't live for
ever, and you won't find a fine gentleman
who'll marry your father's daughter. Don't be
a fool, Ursula. Come with me and I'll see
that you get on; you were made for the stage,
I tell you; we shall secure you an engagement,
never fear; and all London will be raving
about you in a week. Choose which you will
take."

"I cannot answer you now. Give me time
—a little time—to think. How can I speak
now?"

"Why the devil not? Look here; I can't
afford to have any nonsense. Money I must

have, and you must get it me, one way or the other."

" Not that other way, not that."

" Well then, come. Gad, one would think there had never been a girl on the stage before. What's there to shrink from ? Don't be so d—d squeamish." Ursula trembled. " Well then," said Lorton, with the air of one indulging in most undeserved magnanimity, " we won't talk about the stage. There's other things a girl with her wits about her can do."

" Give me time. I will see you again, but I cannot decide now," said Ursula, her voice still trembling.

" There goes Paston," said Lorton, as the hall-door banged. He went to the window, and watched the doctor walking away. " Well, just as you like. We'll close the interview, on the understanding that negotiations are going to proceed. Good-bye, my dear. What, not even a farewell kiss ? Ah well, you'll know better soon. Good-bye." And he left the room.

Poor Ursula. When her father had gone she remained without moving, silent and wretched. She could not go down to tea ; they did not expect her, supposing her to be at the Daltons', where she had talked of going that afternoon. Her brain was in a ferment. What should she

do? Whither should she turn for counsel or
comfort?—to Joanna? That would but give the
dear soul needless pain. How could Joanna
help her in this strait? She knew now—
Lorton's brutal words had brought it home to
her consciousness, so that she felt what she had
hardly suspected before—that help and protection might have come from one man, and he
had deserted her. Even had he not, how should
she dare appeal to him now? What should
she do?

Why should she accept her father's dictation?
He had no rights over her. Ah, but how he
might make some of those she loved suffer.
Rather than that she would buy their happiness
with her own tears. And then the vision of what
life under her father's roof would mean rose
before her mind: the men she would be forced
to meet, the words she would have to hear, the
ill deeds of which she must become aware.
Could she bear it? For a little while she
might; but with what hope? Her father had
said truly she could never marry; how could
she suffer one whom she loved to take the black
burden of her father's guilt upon his shoulders?
Did Arnold know already,—Lorton had said he
knew him,—and was that the reason of his
strange disappearance? No, no; she would
never believe that of him; but she must not

think of him now. Regrets for what might have
been were vain.

What should she do then ? To whom should
she turn ? With pitiful iteration the questions
recurred, still without answer. Suddenly the
ring on her finger caught her attention—her
mother's ring. What would her mother have
her do ? She rose and took from its resting-place
the letter she had received on her birthday, five
short days ago. Five days ! It might have been
five years. Ursula felt as though more suffering
had been compressed into this one week than
she had known in all her life before. She sat
down again with the letter in her hand. Poor
mother ! It was not hard to understand that
she had found her lot unbearable. " Poor
mother ! " Ursula whispered, and kissed the
letter before she opened it. She read till she
came to the words " I will not defend myself
for deserting him." " Ah, mother, mother," said
Ursula, " you little thought how soon I should
learn what slight defence you needed." Her
tears almost broke forth afresh, but she held
them back, and went on reading. " Humbly
grieving for the past "—what a mockery the words
seemed, as applied to this man who had just left
her. " If I have wronged him then, not rightly
perceiving what to do, or how to serve you both,
be yours the privilege of redressing the injury."

Wronged him ?  How could she have wronged
him ?    And yet—yet—might it not have been
otherwise with him if she had stayed by him ?
Might not her influence have turned him in the
course of years?   "It was for my sake she left
him," thought Ursula; "perhaps I am to blame
after all.   Poor mother, she had to choose
between us, and she choose me ; but is there
not still a debt unpaid ?   It may be there was
a wrong in so leaving him.   Is it to be my task
to redress the wrong ?"

So pondered Ursula sitting alone, while the
streets beneath grew empty, and the light faded
out of the sky, and the grey sea down below
grew black, and the waves beat on the beach
with their steady sullen roar.

Lorton had reconnoitred carefully on leaving
the room ; and he slipped down-stairs and out
of the house unseen.   Once outside he turned and
looked up at the windows.

"You're not broken yet," he said, "but broken
you shall be before I've done with you ; and
every stab I give you shall go home to that
woman's heart too.   I shall have you well within
my clutches soon ; and then, by G—! see if I
don't make you do as I say ;" and he moved
along with an evil scowl on his face.

The post-office clerks and their sweethearts
had been taking a Sunday stroll, and they passed

him unnoticed. They stopped and nudged each other with solemn faces, then whispered to the young ladies, who promptly turned and gazed after Lorton's retreating figure.

"Lor!" they all ejaculated in unison, and proceeded tea-wards.

# CHAPTER VI.

## GIBBINS TAKES OFF HIS COAT.

"Oh, that day of sorrow, misery, and rage
I shall carry to the catacombs of age,
Photographically lined
On the tablets of my mind,
When a yesterday has faded from its page!"
*Prince Agib.*

"Methinks I had him thar."—*A. Ward.*

AMONG the many mysterious phenomena of the human mind, there are few more puzzling than the way in which the solution of a problem flashes suddenly into our heads when we have ceased to think of the problem itself. From the day when Archimedes leaped from his bath and fled in primitive attire past the startled attendants through crowded streets to the thronged market-place, crying, "Eureka! Eureka!"—by the way, where were the police, who ought to have stopped him?—men have vainly sought to fathom the secrets of unconscious cerebration. What school-boy does not know how, when exams. are over and done, and he finds that five more marks would have secured him his promotion, the answer to a miserable question which he had left untouched occurs to him, and he curses examinations for being " all luck "? Who has not conversed with an unknown stranger who seemed rather put out by his observations, and a week later remembered with a groan, as he turned over in bed preparatory to going to sleep, that the stranger was Smith whom he met once before at Jones's, and who was reputed the author of that anonymous publication which he had been abusing?

Even so it befell with Joshua Gibbins, when in the midst of his defence before Mrs. Marchpane he was stricken with a Great Idea. Heedless of that good lady's parting shaft, he betook himself with unwonted swiftness to the solitude of his own den, there to turn the Idea over and over, and inspect it on every side, in every possible light. That Idea itself was nothing less than the explanation of the robbery.

Arrived in his sanctum, Joshua sat down in front of the fire, and presently addressed the attentive walls—the best of listeners, by the way, because we have it on good authority that they have ears, and presumably, therefore, hear, while the most garrulous of us may feel confident that they will not interrupt.

"Ed'ard. There now, who'd 'a thought it?

A skittish lookin' chap he wur too. An' to think as it wur that chap! an' yet," said Mr. Gibbins, as he "rubbed an elongated forehead with a meditative cuff," "I dun see as it could ha' bin any one else. Chap must ha' knowed the 'ouse. Well, didn't Ed'ard? Must ha' kep' precious quiet. Well, didn't Ed'ard? Must ha' knowed as Mr. Arnold wur away. Well, that's him agin: didn't Ed'ard?"

Joshua rose and poked the fire to give vent to his feelings; then he stood with the poker in his hand, and spoke winged words to the window.

"An' fur why wur Mr. Arnold a-axin' of his name? Why but because he'd gone an' guessed it too? That wur why! Cattle-oggin'!"

Here a new light broke in upon our friend which required time for realisation. "Jimminy!" he murmured, "an' that 'ere Rock as purtended to be so mighty plucky with his pistols an' firearms a-surprisin' folks at them hours! He wur in it too, an' it were all a bloomin' sell. Him a gammonin' me with his Confusers an' long-winded chaps! Jest for all the world as if I'd bin as green as—as a cabbage."

Mr. Gibbins began to feel hot at this notion, and the housekeeper's taunts recurred to him. "Dull comp'ny fur that chap, as sot there an' talked 's if butter wouldn't melt in his mouth?

Me dull comp'ny? Who'd a thought as I was sittin' a hob-nobbin' with a chap as was only a-waitin' to prig? Me dull comp'ny? 'specks I'll give him some more o' my comp'ny afore we've done. Mrs. Marchpane, mum, much obligated to you I'm sure fur your opinion," quoth he, addressing the absent housekeeper with fine irony, " but you don't know me yet, not by a long way. I'll take the change out o' Rock, mum, or my name ain't Joshua Gibbins. Thought he could make a fool o' me, did he? Wery good. Jest you wait—an' you'll see." And the honest bailiff turned in the fulness of his heart, and smote the coals with the poker in a manner which would have impressed a casual spectator with the feeling that Mr. Rock was likely to have an exceedingly uncomfortable time of it when he next met Mr. Gibbins.

In accordance with the resolution implied in the concluding words of the soliloquy, our wrathful philosopher started a few days later on an expedition to Copesbury, without saying a word of his purpose to the housekeeper. As he travelled, he pondered over the forthcoming interview, during those periods when he was not engaged in exchanging amenities with his companions in the train.

It was not till he had alighted on the platform at his journey's end that he bethought him of his ignorance of Mr. Rock's address. This difficulty, however, was easily got over; and with cheerful anticipations he wended his stately way to the regions where the bookshop was to be found.

Arnold's visit had left the bookseller in a very uncomfortable frame of mind. But the old gentleman's spirits were elastic, and by this morning he felt almost cheerful. Young Robur could hardly mean to come down hard on him now, or he would not have refrained from running him in as a conclusion to the interview. But his feelings received a slight shock, it must be owned, when on descending to the shop, in answer to certain marked sounds intimating the presence of an impatient customer, he found Mr. Joshua Gibbins awaiting him. What did this portend? Nothing, at any rate, he felt, could be lost by urbanity. The light in the shop prevented him from distinguishing his visitor's expression, as that worthy's back was turned to the window.

"Mr. Gibbins? allow me to express my gratification at seeing you again in such apparently excellent health. Are you the bearer of a missive from Mr. Robur? Has he given you any message for me?" The bookseller's tone was more than bland; it was obsequious.

"He hain't," was the laconic answer.

"Not?" cried Mr. Rock, the submissive tone
vanishing from his voice, and being replaced by
one of cordial hilarity : "why, then, it must be
pure good-will that has brought you beneath
my humble roof.    Mr. Gibbins, you do me
honour.   I may indeed say that others, even
among the aristocracy, have acted with similar
kindly regard for my modest merits.   There
was the Marquis of Muddington used to visit
me frequently, I remember, in more prosperous
days.   But that may pass.   I am sure, Mr.
Gibbins, that you have not come here as a
purchaser, but simply as a friend to remind
me of that memorable evening at Oakleigh.
Come, step up-stairs ; let me lead the way to
my sanctum, my parlour, my den ; and with a
good fire and a fifteen inch churchwarden, you
shall be as comfortable as—as in your own
home."

The bailiff was overwhelmed.   Mr. Rock's
volubility made his head reel—he became scarcely
responsible for his actions.   He followed his host
in silence from sheer inability to get out a word.
He even suffered the garrulous elder to fill a pipe
for him and thrust him into a chair by a roaring
fire before he found himself able to speak.   And
then he was only capable of ejaculating,

" Jimminy ! "

" *Gemini*, the twins, as they taught me in my

young days. I knew you were a wise man, Mr.
Gibbins, but I was not aware that you were also
a Latin scholar. You refer, I suppose, with
singular subtlety and aptness to the fact that
our mutual feelings might be compared to those
of twin brothers ? A pretty idea, very pretty,
and not altogether unlike one that our late Bishop,
good worthy man, once produced in this very
pulpit at the Cathedral. If I remember rightly,
he owed the suggestion to me ; for he was fond
of dropping in for a chat—but there, I'm talking
about old acquaintances again. Excuse me ; but
as we get old we get talkative, Mr. Gibbins."

The bailiff puffed spasmodically at his pipe.
His manner was a little puzzling to Mr. Rock,
who still did not feel quite sure that there might
not be something up. He resolved to try a new
tack.

" How is that excellent lady, Mrs. Marchpane ?
I trust she is well. It is really singular how
much she reminded me of the Duchess of ——— ;
but there, I forget. A man of your insight and
discrimination must appreciate and be appreciated
by a woman of such superior intelligence ; and
indeed I must say that I should not suspect Miss
Rhoda of being deficient in that respect either ;
and a comely young woman she is too—but that
is neither here nor there, as we men of the world
know, Mr. Gibbins, eh ? Beauty fades ; virtue

becomes stale, flat, and unprofitable, as the
Psalmist says. It is Brains, sir, Brains that rule
the world, as you and I know!"

What was to be answered to such flattery as
was here artfully implied? The honest sage of
Oakleigh was positively dazed by the shower-
bath of words which deluged his ears. But the
reference to Mrs. Marchpane stirred him.

"Mrs. Marchpane, sir, is a woman as hev her
wits about her; but seein' as Prov'dence hev seen
fit to make her jest a woman an' no more, what's
the use? 'Uman natur'? Much she knows of
'Uman natur'! 'preciate? Maybe she do, but
she takes the rummiest way o' shewin' it as
ever I see. Blest if she didn't say as I wur dull
comp'ny! What d'ye think o' that?" And
Joshua having thus unbosomed himself, relapsed
into silence. His speech had already attained
to some length; he required, so to speak, fresh
supplies of water to produce the necessary steam
for a farther outbreak.

"Dull company? My dear sir! she couldn't
have meant it—impossible. You will never persuade me to believe, Mr. Gibbins, that man,
woman, or child outside of a lunatic asylum
could have dreamed of applying such an expression to you. And an intelligent woman like
that! Come, you must have misunderstood her.
Even the most lucid of speakers are sometimes

misunderstood—Mr. Gladstone, for instance, not to mention myself," said Mr. Rock with complacent self-depreciation. "Now it was just such a little bit of misunderstanding that set the worthy Earl of Widdling and his wife quarrelling, till they all but got separated; when somebody suggested that there was something wrong. Then it turned out that when he thought she had been abusing him, she had only been abusing somebody else who was his own pet aversion ; and so they made it up again. And I'll undertake to say that Mrs. Marchpane's remark was capable of being as easily explained. And at any rate, what matters it to us, who are philosophers, what the ladies think of us ? Of course, we would like the sweet creatures to be careful of our creature comforts; but if those are secure, what matters ? The dear souls haven't our opportunities, and if I may say so without a breach of becoming modesty, my dear sir, they haven't our brains either." And Mr. Rock chuckled, and leaned across to his companion to point the remark by a gentle pat on the knee.

"Mr. Rock," said Gibbins in a dignified tone, "I'll trouble you to drop it. It's wery true, all as you say, no doubt, but, I've heard it afore ; an' what's more, I could ha' said it myself. An' my knees was not made for slappin', neither fur

the gen'ral public, so to speak, to be a makin' free
with.   Drop it."

The bookseller was surprised greatly by this
address.   He imagined that he had established
himself thoroughly in the other's good graces,
and the awakening was rude.   But he thought
he was more than a match for his rustic friend.

" Mr. Gibbins," he said, drawing himself up,
" I do not understand your language.   What are
you at ? "

" What 'm I at ?   Ah, yes.   Jest you do a bit
o' thinkin', an' you'll know what I'm at.   I ain't
come here fur nothin'.   Joshua Gibbins don't go
a-loafin' about without he means it—you rest
upon me fur that."

The precise meaning of this harangue was
exceedingly recondite ; Joshua unluckily had an
astonishing disregard for grammar.   But the
general drift was fairly obvious.   The bookseller
felt that his guest had not come to Copesbury
merely to smoke the pipe of peace in his den.

" I didn't expect this from you when I seated
you in that chair, Mr. Gibbins.   You forget yourself, it appears.   If you have no more control
over your feelings than the late Marquis, you
had better adjourn.   I assure you I have no
desire to thrust myself into the society of persons who are unable to appreciate the fruits of
long experience on both sides of the herring

pond; but I will not be insulted in my own house by a man—yes, by Jingo, a man with my own pipe in his mouth!"

Gibbins paused in his smoking open-mouthed, and cogitated. Then he turned his thoughts into acts with calm deliberation. He broke his pipe in half, arranged the end of it which had been in his mouth carefully under his heel, and scrunched it. Then he deposited the other half on the top of the fire, and drove it home in leisurely wise; and lastly, leaned forward in his chair, and spoke in measured accents.

"Pipe? bless you, there's your pipe — a-scrunched."

Mr. Rock felt that this was adding insult to injury. He resolved to scath this provincial party.

"Thank you, Mr. Gibbins: you remind me that it is scarcely becoming for me to talk to a low-bred animal like you. Why, blest if the chap doesn't think he's got brains! Lord, he thinks he knows what he's doing—as if any soul would condescend to have any dealings with such an ass—*such* an ass—unless he saw his way to immediate profit. Man alive, you're the blimiest fool I ever set eyes on! Clear out of here! off with you!"

This strife of philosophers would have been a god-send to Lucian.

Mr. Gibbins rose slowly, and unbuttoned the breast of his coat. It then appeared that he contemplated divesting himself of that article. Could it be that he had an assault in view ? Mr. Rock was alarmed by the idea. He imagined that the stolid bailiff would be overwhelmed, and lack the requisite energy for farther proceedings. To leave the room was impossible : he rapidly ensconced himself behind a table.

Joshua removed his coat, and laid it carefully on a chair ; then he turned round.

" Here," cried Rock, " I say, what are you going to do ? I was only joking, really I was, honour bright."

The bailiff disregarded this address. He eyed Rock behind his rampart. " I am a-goin'," he observed, " to let you see as I got somethin' to say."

The meaning of this euphemism was clear. Rock thought it time to try and shout for assistance. " Murder ! " he exclaimed.

The other paused. This was a line of defence he had not reckoned on. But he soon decided what was to be done.

" If you holler," he said peacefully, " I'll knock your pesky old head off." He followed up the remark by heaving the table out of his way. Then before Mr. Rock had time for a

scream, his head was suddenly placed in chancery.
He struggled, but it was vain. The hand of
Fate was descending on him, not without evidence of considerable animus on the part of the
remorseless goddess.

" Gr—umph—hi—help ! O Lor ! "

" Come, what's going on here ? Gibbins ! "

The combatants parted. Panting and dishevelled, the bookseller fled behind his table
again.

" Now then, Gibbins, what's all this ? What
on earth are you doing ? " The speaker, Mr.
Armitage, who had thus opportunely appeared
on the scenes, seemed, it must be owned, more
amused than indignant at the spectacle to which
he found himself a witness.

Gibbins saluted the clergyman apologetically.
" Axin' your pardon, Mr. Armitage, sir, but I
wur jest a-takin' the change out o' this chap
fur his owdacious cheek, as come to Oakleigh
a-cattle-oggin', an' all fur why ? Why in course,
to see if there warn't nothin' as he could prig.
An' him a-sittin' in my room, a-talkin' as if
butter wouldn't melt in his mouth, an' jest been
a-cheekin' of me now till there ! I couldn't ha'
kep' from 'ittin' of him, not if you'd been in the
room yourself, sir."

Armitage could hardly refrain from laughing.
" Well," he said, " I should think you'd got

enough change out of him by now for all his
offences. He doesn't look happy. Now I think
you had better go—or you may feel obliged to
hit him again; and I can't have that. You had
no business to do it at all, Gibbins. That will
do. Leave Mr. Rock to me. Good day."

Gibbins had put on his coat again in the
interval.

"Well, sir," he said with dignity, "mebbe I
wur wrong. But there—I'd like to do it agin.
Makes me feel as if there wur a brighter side
arter all. Good day, sir." And the bailiff with-
drew, deigning only a haughty glance in the
direction of the chastised bookseller.

The Canon's interview with Rock was short.
He had been commissioned by Arnold, who had
gone up to town, to undertake the settlement
of that worthy, to whom he communicated the
fact that Mr. Robur had resolved to let him off
without farther punishment for reasons of his
own, adding that the condition was that he
should remain at Copesbury on his good behaviour,
as any signs of irregularity would result in his
being handed over to the police. He was to be
allowed to retain his present quarters, under the
eye of the Canon.

"And I must say, I don't think you deserve
to be let off in that way," said Armitage, as he
opened the door to depart; "though perhaps

the account is pretty well squared by the inter-view I interrupted just now. Dishonesty doesn't seem to have paid you better than it usually does. Let me recommend you to try honesty for a change."

# CHAPTER VII.

## GUESSED WRONG.

"May Time, who sheds his blight o'er all,
　And daily dooms some joy to death,
O'er thee let years so gently fall
　They shall not crush one flower beneath!
As half in shade and half in sun
　This world along its path advances,
May that side the sun's upon
　Be all that e'er shall meet thy glances."—*Moore.*

In order to follow the fortunes of our hero we must be prepared to inhale for his sake that unique combination of smoke and grit which the Londoner calls an atmosphere. It may be true, indeed, that there is no other name to call it by ; but that only proves the poverty of the Londoner's invention in still using the same term to describe the genuine article and its spurious substitute.

It was the second evening after Paston's return from Burnport, and he was just pulling off his boots after a hard day's work, preparatory to solacing his weary soul with tobacco, when he stopped and growled :—

"Well, if that isn't the —$n^{th}$ time I've heard that bell to-day!"

The vexation which had occasioned the somewhat exaggerated mathematical precision of this remark was turned into the keenest joy when the door opened and disclosed Robur, portmanteau in hand.

The two friends stared at each other blankly for a moment, and then burst simultaneously into a duet of laughter.

"Ungird thyself, my wandering Odysseus," cried the doctor, shoving Arnold into a chair. "Where in the name of goodness have you been hiding all this time?"

"My dear fellow, how should I know? I was at home for a while, I fancy, and then Armitage housed me at Copesbury."

He spoke uncomfortably. His associations with Paston were so entirely pleasant that the first glimpse of the doctor had made him forget everything but his delight at their meeting; his merriment had been spontaneous and unalloyed while it lasted.

Associations are responsible for a good many of our vagaries. It is recorded that a certain pedagogue, lecturing one day upon the Greek Testament, invited his class to "turn to the *Blessed Original*," by which apt designation he intended to refer to our English Version of the same. Peradventure it was not the first time that a translation has been credited with authenticity !

Arnold's brooding sadness had only relinquished its hold for an instant, and now settled down upon him again as he took his eyes off Paston's face.

" Well, I see you've come to stay," observed that cheerful person, seizing his friend's portmanteau and giving it to a servant outside with directions for its owner's accommodation.

" Now," he said, as he returned and closed the door, " while they're getting some supper for us I'll tell you a piece of news. To begin with, then, I've been down at Burnport at your house of call to look for you. Not finding you, I stayed a day or so, and made the acquaintance of your friends at East Rise. What do you think of that ? "

The doctor's hearer apparently thought a good deal of it. He looked as if he were beginning to grow interested.

" I don't know exactly what business it was that took you away from the place in such a hurry," continued Paston, " so if by accident I happen to jump heavily on your feelings you must forgive me."

" For God's sake go on; you probably know more about the business, whatever it is, than I do."

Arnold was excited. Could he have made a mistake that night when he last saw Ursula? Was Paston going to prove to him that he had been the victim of a mere optical illusion? Impossible : he had never told the doctor the history of the case. And yet nothing less than such an explanation could do him any good. No ; he could not expect to hear anything of real importance. However, he would make certain.

"You saw Miss Lorton ? " he interrupted, just as the other was beginning.

" Yes, and liked her immensely."

There was something exquisitely humorous about this unconscious irony, and Arnold emitted a sound that was midway between a laugh and a groan.

" Humph ! er—how do you like the way she dresses ? "

Paston concealed his astonishment at this question with rare presence of mind as he replied,—

" Very much. I never saw tasteful simplicity set off to greater advantage."

" Simplicity ! " (" He's very bad," thought the doctor.) " Why, she hasn't left off wearing jewellery, has she ? " enquired Arnold in a manner that was very obviously forced.

" I don't think she had any on when I saw her," returned the other innocently. " Yes, she had though," he exclaimed, correcting himself after a short pause for reflection. " I remember noticing that she wore a rather handsome ring on her left hand."

" Just so ; but I'm afraid my stupid questions have made you wander rather from what you are going to tell me. Please clear up my anxiety on that point before we talk about anything else."

Arnold's voice was oddly at variance with the eagerness he professed to feel. He had lapsed into a cold calm tone all of a sudden, as if what he said was purely a matter of form.

" There's a pretty little complication going on down there," said Paston, nodding his head mysteriously, and ignoring his companion's evident want of interest. " Miss Joanna Blunsden is in the thick of it, and she has taken me into her confidence, with permission to impart the whole story to you."

He bent forward in his chair towards Arnold, and added in a low voice :—" I daresay you are unaware of it, but Miss Lorton's father has —turned up alive."

Thereupon he described minutely all that was known of Lorton's career, and identified him with " the long-lost brother," whom his hearer re- membered to have seen haunting the parade at Burnport. He went on to relate how this adventurer was scheming to get possession of his daughter, the energy and devotion of one brave woman being all that intervened to save her from his cruel clutches.

"We talked a long time, but could find no way out of it. Lord knows if he mayn't have succeeded by now," said Paston, when he had finished the tale.

Arnold was thoroughly roused: his lips quivered and his teeth ground together as he realized Ursula's dependence upon strangers to shield her from one who should have been her best friend—her own father. She must soon know all, if she had not been told already, and then he would take her away with him from her home, the healthy innocence of her present occupations, the friendship of the few people whom she was learning to love, above all she would lose Aunt Joan's companionship at the very time when she had but just arrived at a full appreciation of it. One feeble link to connect her with the past might remain in the person of Frank; or would he, on discovering the truth, break with her of his own accord? Lorton would be certain to do all in his power to promote the marriage, as the best thing for him would be a wealthy and tractable son-in-law. A luxurious residence in some foreign watering-place, a life sweetened by filial caresses,—and filial credit,—these were among the benefits to be secured by appropriating Mr. Dalton's son; how was it possible to suppose that Lorton had neglected or overlooked them. The only question was whether the veteran intriguer would succeed in keeping Frank to his engagement, especially as his daughter was sure to release her lover, and might even press him to consider his own interests by leaving her.

Supper was consumed by the pair almost in silence, which was not broken till it had been cleared away, and they were left to themselves.

" It is curious how fruitful in discoveries last Sunday was," observed Paston very deliberately, selecting a pipe from his rack with critical impartiality; "you would scarcely believe it, perhaps, but I made one on my own account. My hat! talk about a foul pipe!" and he hastily laid down the offending utensil, and began to search for another.

At last he was suited sufficiently to pick up the thread where he had dropped it.

" You remember I mentioned having seen that fellow Lorton just for a moment: I wonder how many aliases he can boast, by the way. Well, whom do you think I recognized in him? Some-one you have seen and spoken to yourself."

Arnold's heart beat wildly as Paston answered his own question:

" Edwards! Edwards late of the *Tuba*,—for I

happen to know that he's been out of that for some time. Why, man, what's the matter ? "

Arnold struck his hands together and sprang out of his chair. Who would have thought it ? The doctor's news had turned out to be of supreme importance after all.

It was now Arnold's turn, and he related the revelations of the secret drawer, and the appearance of its missing contents upon Ursula's finger.

"The connexion between the ring and Miss Lorton's father is certainly clear enough," commented the doctor, "but I don't see my way to tracing it farther than his possession ; he couldn't have given it to her without Miss Joanna's knowledge, even had it been possible to induce Miss Lorton to accept it without revealing himself and his claims to her."

There is a fatal tendency to get bewildered over somewhat intricate problems of any sort; but when such problems relate to human nature, where scarcely any of the conditions necessary for solution can be considered as ascertained, it is owing rather to good luck than personal capacity that answers ever come out right. Paston and Robur both hailed from a University which is justly famed for the prominence. of mathematics among its prescribed studies. Yet it may be affirmed that a senior wrangler would not have stood a better chance of rightly comprehending the ins and outs of the difficulty than either of these honest bunglers.

"I fear it is only too easy to see how the ring got to her," said Arnold sadly; "it did not come directly, but through another person—Frank Dalton."

Paston's incredulity was displayed in his wide-opened eyes and a gesture of his hands.

"He has forestalled me," persisted Arnold. "I might have forgiven him this," he touched the scar on his forehead; "but—well, I suppose he had a perfect right to do it, though the same cannot be said of the physical pain which he inflicted. Anyhow, he had no right to economize at my expense in the matter of procuring an engagement ring. I had scarcely suspected them of caring very seriously for each other before my last evening at Burnport, though he had been confoundedly in the way for some time. I thought it was only his awkward, witless nature that prevented him from seeing how he must bore her by dogging her about so; only he didn't bore her, it seems; and I was wrong about it altogether. That night my suspicions were aroused by the way in which they kept apart from the others. Then I caught a glimpse of the ring, my poor mother's ring,—I could swear to it,—and after that——"

"You threw up the sponge," said the doctor metaphorically, concluding poor Arnold's unfinished sentence for him. "Ah; do you think Master Frank had anything to do with pilfering your bureau, then?" he proceeded, trying to look as if the case was interesting to him mainly from an abstract point of view, and not for any personal concern which he might happen to feel in his friend's happiness.

"I can hardly help doing so," was the reply; "the arguments seem to me overwhelming. Just think what they are: I find evidence that convicts two men of having rifled my cabinet during my absence from home; I go to one of those men to charge him with having taken the ring; in his confusion he fancies that I know more than I do, and then I find out indirectly that Frank Dalton was instigated by the others to shoot me. Surely he must have had some motive of his own for them to turn to account. Mere dislike would not drive him to such an extreme, so I am bound to assume that it was partly terror at the thought of his complicity in the theft being discovered, and that Rock and Edwards fostered this feeling in their pupil to serve their own interests. Then it may well have been that, as they were unable to profitably dispose of the ring with safety, they bribed the young fool with it to murder me, in which case there would have been plenty of circumstantial evidence to convict him, and nothing against them but his discredited word, so long as the drawer held its secrets."

"Yes, I can't say I see any flaw in the argument so far," muttered the doctor reluctantly.

Perhaps it was scarcely unreasonable that Arnold should have at first settled it in his own mind that Frank Dalton was the actual purloiner of the ring. That he was unable to form any notion how the theft had been effected had not deterred him from arriving at this main conclusion. It was the only possible explanation of the facts, he had told himself; and he had clung tenaciously to it, as men will to the unstable fabric of preconceived ideas. To silently impute this fresh crime to Frank was to Arnold an unavoidable breach of charity. Was it likely that the boy would stay his hand from taking a chattel when he had not shrunk from attempting the life of its owner?

Now, however, events had come to light which deepened Arnold's bad opinion of his worthless rival. Instead of being a principal in the ring transaction, it turned out that he had been nothing more than a willing dupe, a creature beside whom the determined villain becomes comparatively an amiable philanthropist. No crime is too wild for a besotted weakling: such a being can pass at one step from drawing-room nonentity to nauseating triumphs in the arena of infamy.

"Next comes the crowning achievement," proceeded Arnold; "he disposes of the ring in a way that makes it as impossible for me to denounce him on that score as it was to expose his former villainy—the villainy that was discovered, though not actually perpetrated, first. There you have the entire case, my friend : nothing is left for me but to hold my tongue and——"

"I can't understand the audacity of that infernal young scoundrel," broke out Paston hotly; "why, if your view of him is correct, I never knew before what a hardened criminal was; and yet I don't see any other view to take, unless we are to believe that he shot at you without any motive at all, in which case he must be mad. Suppose he really is mad, now ! Couldn't you have him watched ?"

"You talk as if I were a regular melodramatic villain myself, Paston ;" and Arnold smiled dolefully. "I shall know where to get one signature, at any rate, if I ever want to concoct a certificate for the incarceration of an inconvenient relative. No, no," he went on ; "it is a melancholy and provoking fact, but he is not a bit mad ; only weak."

Next day Arnold, needing distraction, found it in walking about London.

It was an occupation which possessed many attractions for him, though he seldom got an opportunity of thus indulging himself. Walking with a companion is well enough, if the companion is agreeable; but then the enjoyment is merely that of good company, and the fact of being on one's legs all the time quite a secondary matter. A walk to be thoroughly appreciated for its own sake must be taken in solitude; the seclusion must not be broken by more than a passing greeting. The sincere and single-minded pedestrian will have no *téte-à-téte*, except that absorbing one with Nature. He is unsociable to the extent of allowing no one to button-hole him when he is out alone with his mistress, or divert his mind from her. Tourists and loungers —two opposite extremes—can do as they like; walking being less their object than the achievement of distances in the one case, and the society of acquaintances in the other. A man is not bound to walk for the sake of walking; but should he do so, he must become a genuine hermit for the time. His mental attitude—for it is not to the mere physical exertion but to the ethics of walking that allusion is here made —his mind must change its mien with his body. Knowing that these two parts of him are naturally interdependent, he dislikes to set them at variance by not allowing them to keep step

together when his body takes the air : as if the
soul had no accommodating gait of its own, or
were without the means of adjusting it.

Descending Paston's doorsteps, Arnold ceased
to play the first part on his own limited stage,
and became at once an ordinary spectator of, or
at any rate an unnoticed " walking gentleman "
in, the pageant of humanity ; since it is not
possible for anyone to avoid being a more or
less active member of that company. He hailed
with pleasure the chance this subordinate position
gave him of observing how other " supers " com-
ported themselves. For, if the truth must be
told, he was getting not a little tired of his own
affairs, and, unlike Milton's Satan, greatly preferred serving in heaven, as this wider sphere
was by comparison, to ruling a small and select
hell in undisturbed privacy.

Not that he was by any means a town mouse ;
on the contrary, he revelled in country scenery.
Mountains, gentler undulations, plains with their
unobtrusive fertility, forest and lake, fell and
fen, were sights with which he could boast an
intimacy denied to most even of those who are
in the habit of visiting such places. But just as
there are emotions which respond to the various
combinations of external Nature, and just as
localities differ in the suggestions they supply
to the fancy, so there are certain moods which

urgently demand to be propitiated by appropriate sights and sounds. A rustic homestead chimes in with a feeling of placid contentment better than a humming thoroughfare. Elbowing and being elbowed, hustling and being hustled : that is a state of things not conducing to placidity. Such a predilection must be gratified by leisure, ample room, and the host of simple pleasures which make up one's modest ideal of life in the country. So strong is the fostering influence of these surroundings, indeed, that what is only a passing whim to start with may be reared into a confirmed and permanent unfitness for urban society and pursuits.

Streets, too, have their fascination, appealing to many restless and not ignoble frames of mind. A man may be as devout a lover of Nature as any, and yet feel himself at home here, and not in the presence of inarticulate creation alone. Or rather it may be said that the streets themselves are inarticulate, their burden not being so easy of comprehension from the confused hubbub of echoes caused by the crowds which pace or hurry through them. For Nature, extruded from her fields and hedgerows by the advancing lines of brick and mortar, doffs her green mantle and returns, tenfold more vigorous in her new guise.

Arnold found himself in Oxford Street, and

paused to consider whither he should tend his
steps. With the West End and its sharp, sometimes revolting, contrasts he had some acquaintance, picked up on various occasions when he
had stayed with friends in town. But of the
East he knew nothing: so he set off to walk
there.

Crossing the boundary of fashion which lies
somewhere between Oxford Circus and Totten-
ham Court Road, he was soon past the hollow-
eyed gentility and intellectual exclusiveness of
Bloomsbury (not that this last is the fault of
Bloomsbury or its institutions). The outlying
strongholds and ambushes of the law came
next, some of them almost deserted by their
legal owners—legal in one sense only, however:
for rents are still paid for the chambers in and
about Holborn much the same as elsewhere,
for all the kindly efforts of socialist reformers to
remove this antiquated encumbrance of tenancy.
He threaded his way through the City, moved
to a quicker pace by the complacent ostentation
of the paradise of vulgarity, so grotesquely at
variance with the dignity of its architectural
surroundings. He noticed, too, as being a
scarcely less characteristic feature of the place,
the vast amount of eating and drinking without
which business cannot now-a-days be conducted.
It was not till he reached the end of Leadenhall

Street, and debouched into Aldgate just where a few antique gables have hitherto managed to survive, that Arnold slackened his speed and began to breathe freely again. He emerged upon the region of tramways, and looked about him in this strange quarter with keen interest.

Everything was new: he was surprised to find Whitechapel not at all the repulsive neighbourhood he had expected. In spite of the greater density of the population, the reeking courts and alleys, the flood of life that roared down the main channels, receiving tributary rivulets at every turn,—in spite too of the endless variety of pursuits from brewing to rag-picking,—the contrasts, though they were more numerous, were not jarringly obvious as in the parts just traversed. The very sameness took his fancy, for it was of a kind to which he was totally unaccustomed. The copiousness of material, indeed, overwhelmed his imagination at first; but presently he grew less bewildered, and longed to know more about this seething mass of humanity from which his past experience separated him so effectually even while he mingled with it.

The London Hospital with its plain comfortable appearance was left in the rear now, and the quaint alms-houses that stand back from the road wearing an almost irresistible look of

invitation upon their queer old faces.  Down
the Mile End Road and its begrimed terraces,
where the houses look out with dim gloomy
eyes upon rank grass plots and blackened trees,
to the canal - bridges of Bow, till the hoary
church opposes its scarred brick bosom to the
ceaseless rush of traffic, a mute protest for which
the triumphant Spirit of Commerce makes con-
temptuous allowance by dividing its forces, with
orders to pursue two separate courses at this
point, one on each side of the venerable obstacle,
and not to bear it down incontinently.  So on
to Stratford, almost the only interesting thing
about which modernized suburb is that it occupies
a famous site.  How this Stratford—the Stratford of cheap brick facings and an absurdly
pretentious town - hall — how this vastly im-
proved and enlightened district would turn up
its nose now at the wretched old "Stratford
atte Bowe" which it has so completely dispos-
sessed and effaced.  Who would dare to speak
slightingly now of the Parisian accent which
may be acquired (terms moderate) at its young
ladies' seminaries ?

Arnold turned into a confectioner's shop, and
continued his meditations over a cup of tea
and a roll.  Why should he not try the experiment of taking up a temporary abode in these
oriental slums ?  He thought about this till the

idea took firm hold of him : he resolved to make
enquiries about any social movement that might
happen to be already on foot there, and in need
of active adherents. The era of Toynbee Hall
and the extension of the Underground Railway
eastwards was still to come when Arnold formed
this plan. Unselfish labour was exactly the
thing wanted for him, and he hailed the prospect
of getting work so entirely congenial : he would
consult Paston about it.

He started to walk back. Tramping along
the pavement, however, is tiring work : moreover, on this particular occasion the wind set
dead in our pedestrian's teeth, driving minute
particles of dirt into eyes, nose, and mouth.
At last he could bear it no longer : a tram-car
was passing, and he took shelter in it.

There were a good many passengers ; that
was all he observed as he took the nearest
vacant seat.

"I beg your pardon ; I hope I'm not in your
way," said Arnold, for the individual next him
had started violently, and was edging away from
him in an uncomfortable fashion.

The man made no reply ; but, as Arnold
turned to look at him in some surprise, he rose
hastily and left the car.

There was no misunderstanding this action ; it
was due to mutual and instantaneous recognition.

It was not the first time that Robur and
Lorton had met, nor was it the intention of the
latter gentleman that it should be the last.
There were circumstances, however, which placed
a person of his refined susceptibility at a peculiar
disadvantage on the present occasion ; he wanted
to be surer of the hand his intended son-in-law
proposed to play before he could take much
pleasure in his society.  Hence his sudden and
considerate exit.

Arnold did not attempt to follow.  To his
mind, weakened by ill health and suffering,
the occurrence only served to strengthen his
inclination to acquaint himself more closely
with the East End.  It was clear that Ursula's
father had his quarters there, and he had a
vague notion that by living in the same neighbourhood he might be of service to Ursula.
She had Frank to protect her, to be sure ; and
Lorton would be unlikely to burden himself
with keeping her, as long as others were willing
to bear the expense.  Arnold could not bear to
think of her living with her father in Whitechapel, and rejoiced to feel that there could be
no danger of that ever coming to pass while
Aunt Joan was alive.  Still, the fancy took him
of keeping Lorton in sight, should that be
possible, for his child's sake.

When the tide of humanity cast him up once

more at Paston's door he was calm, and even
cheerful. The doctor approved of his design
about looking out for work eastward, and
promised assistance.

"There will be no difficulty about getting
heaps to do out there," said he; "the only
stipulation I make is that you must be quite
well before you undertake it."

Arnold told him about the accidental encounter
in the tram-car.

"And you allowed the brute to escape!
Well, all I can say is that justice would never
be done if such outrageously Quixotic conduct
was the rule," grumbled Paston.

"Think not? Anyhow, I'm going to let
those rogues off, and not bother myself any
more about them. I'm too lazy to take the
necessary proceedings, if you like: only don't
pester me, there's a good fellow."

The other fumed in silence for a minute or
two. When he opened his lips it was only to
remark :

"It's an atrocious piece of foolishness: shake
hands."

"I go up to Cambridge to - morrow," said
Arnold, complying; "I have changed my mind
there so often before that I may do so again,"
he added with a laugh.

Paston eyed his friend grimly.

"One morsel of advice and we'll drop the subject," was his oracular rejoinder: " be careful that no false idea of chivalry and self-effacement leads you to commit a species of moral suicide, that's all."

# CHAPTER VIII.

### UNRESPITED.

" But though this mayde tendre were of age,
Yes in the brest of her virginitee
There was enclosèd rype and sad corage."

*Chaucer.*

Mr. Lorton had laid his plans for his daughter's future happiness well, but he was nevertheless labouring under one or two serious misconceptions. Chief among these was his tacit assumption that "the Blunsden woman" was the only person, except Ursula, who knew him for what he really was. All the rest of his private circle of acquaintances, Robur, Paston, Frank Dalton, Gibbins, even his old friend Hiram Rock, were in possession of a mere portion—in most cases a very small portion—of the facts about himself. He had taken such excellent precautions to conceal the vital incidents in his history, telling only the two persons upon whose silence he thought he could reckon, because their own interests would be hazarded by exposing him, that he was inclined to think very little of his meeting with Arnold in London. It was inconvenient and premature, nothing more.

The happy father had not quitted the repose of the sea-side before he was well assured of his daughter's obedience to his wishes. By dint of adroit manœuvring he had secured another interview with her, at which he experienced the hardly-earned joy of extracting from her lips the promise that she would join him in a few days. That very evening he wrote to her intimating the time and place when and where he should expect her to appear. Commodious lodgings in the neighbourhood of Stepney were already taken, he informed her, and would be in readiness for them the following Monday.

How to inveigle Robur into the toils prepared for him, and induce him to visit " Mr. and Miss Edwards" in their modest retreat, was the only problem that now exercised the ingenuous parental mind.

He hugged himself when he looked back, and thought to what splendid effect he had turned his time at Burnport. He went down there to find out all he could about Robur with the view of removing any ground for the misconstruction which that dull-witted young land-owner might some day be tempted to place on his conduct as the temporary though involuntary possessor of the ring. In this purpose he had been so thoroughly successful that he could confidently anticipate the restoration of the ring in the most delicate way possible to its original owner. Lorton's knowledge of Frank's attachment to Ursula had been of great service to him. He was able to turn it to double account : first as a means of disposing of the ring in a plausible manner; secondly as an occasion of getting Robur out of the way just at the moment when his presence was likely to make matters a little awkward.

The fact that there were two moths scorching their wings in the candle instead of one did not discompose this benevolent schemer. He remarked it as a decidedly useful trait in his daughter's character that she should encourage as many lovers to pay her their addresses simultaneously as could plead pecuniary eligibility to prove their honourable intentions. Ursula was not altogether without his commercial instincts, it seemed : the thought brought a "flattering unction" which Mr. Lorton may have been somewhat hasty in laying to his soul. But his child's prosperity was at stake, and he was not long in deciding between these rival tenders for her affection. Frank might have a larger amount of spare cash in prospect than Arnold had rolling about at the bank to his account now, but then it *was* in prospect only, and not actually guaranteed. Frank was under age, and entirely dependent on his father, whose good intentions might not survive the intelligence of his son's marriage. Breach of promise was quite out of the question as a card to play : even supposing it to be possible for Ursula to be made plaintiff in such a suit and win it, the evidence would certainly involve her parent in undesirable notoriety as the defendant hero of further legal proceedings. The objections against the other candidate for the girl's hand were less insuperable ; what property Robur possessed was entirely under his own control, nor was there anything to hinder it from falling by a natural and informal transfer as entirely under the control of his father-in-law. Besides, how could one forego the rich harvest of revenge which might be reaped by this union of outlawry with respectability ? Mr. Lorton found this last reflection infinitely soothing, and did not long resist its luscious suggestions. He thought of all the scares Arnold had been responsible for causing in his anxious breast and that of his late amiable colleague. His decision was made ; with unselfish magnanimity he resolved that he would bestow his daughter upon the very man from whose malignant persecution he had suffered so much. The determination might have appeared to cost him little, so gleeful was the expression worn by his engaging countenance when he arrived at it. No less remarkable among feats of self-abnegation was the contented way in which he rubbed his hands as he gently murmured,

" A neat little furnace of the best Wallsend flaming cheerfully on the top of his blooming skull would be nothing to it ! "

A strict regard for veracity compels the faithful chronicler to relate that the yearning father's perseverance remained totally unrewarded by outside encouragement. Even the benedictions of conscience, which are supposed to make up in some cases for the chilly regard of popular favour, were denied to him, that usually active monitor having struck work altogether in his case about three-and-twenty years before. It was abundantly evident that Ursula sympathised neither with his aspirations nor with the means by which he pursued them. However incorrect his estimate of his daughter might be, at any rate he could see that she was scarcely in touch with him so far.

Thus it was that the day which saw Arnold depart for Cambridge, with a heart somewhat lightened of its load of doubt, broke upon at least one sorely troubled household at Burnport. The girl had fought out her battle, to be sure ; and but a few hours sufficed to brace her for facing what seemed a quite hopeless fate. Her oppressor's terms were irrevocably accepted now. She had acted alone, upon her own responsibility : there was no choice of ways permitted to her, and—after the first transient acuteness of the shock was over—no craven shrinking, no temporising weakness had interfered to mar her resolution. But it was over : an interval of four clear days was still before her in which to prepare for the future's weary, unremitting sacrifice. Prepare! All the softness in Ursula's nature was stirred to its unknown depths by the word.

Aunt Joan—both the sisters—must be told, for at present they knew nothing, or at least not everything. There had been less intercourse than usual between the members of the little family of late : had each of them been purposely avoiding the others? It seemed so. Further concealment, however, was impossible. Love imposes strict obligations on all who enjoy its treasures, nor was Joanna Blunsden one to turn a deaf ear to its exactions.

Possessed by a consuming desire for support, Ursula strove no longer after the empty consolations of independence, but lost no time in seeking out her one available friend. She found Joanna down-stairs by herself; making a feebler shift than ever to appear profoundly engrossed by ordinary household matters.

" What do you think ? " she began with spasmodic cheerfulness,—then seeing the new expression in Ursula's face she checked herself; and in a moment the two women were clasped in a mute embrace. A long silence, more eloquent than any verbal revelation could have been of the secrets with which the heart of each was overflowing.

" Love casteth out fear," whispered Joanna at last, kissing Ursula upon the forehead.

They sat down, the elder woman where she had been seated over her accounts, the younger on a low arm-chair, almost low enough to be a stool, at the other's feet.

Ursula held Aunt Joan's hand in hers and caressed it fondly.

"I heard it all last Sunday: I have arranged to— to go away, and live with him in London," she said, making a strenuous effort to control her voice.

" My child, my child," murmured Joanna. No mother's moan could have been more piteous.

" It is not yet, dear—not for the greater part of a week, Aunt Joan; only think, the greater part of a week! it might have been so much shorter; " and a smile flickered dimly through the girl's tears, gleaming its faint rainbow message of hope.

Was it faith or infatuation? Joanna hailed the symbol blindly.

" We are not to be parted like this, my child; I will never believe it. No, no; have you grown to be more to me than my own flesh and blood that I can resign you to one who has never given you anything but your name? Why, it is an undeserved hardship for you to be forced to have even that in common with him : as for it giving him any claim to your love, it is enough if it does not make you hate him ! "

" Hush, dear, hush ; don't make it harder for me," moaned Ursula, hiding her face in the folds of Aunt Joan's dress.

The poor woman's heart was wrung. " My own sweet girl " was all she could say as she bent her head down upon those fair disordered tresses, and mingled her own grey hairs with them.

After a while the pang dulled, however, and they were both able to talk more calmly. The passion of grief degenerates into mere selfishness if it is prolonged.

" Perhaps it will not be so bad as it seems at first," said Ursula, looking up again ; " at any rate it would have been worse for me to have left you earlier, would it not? though it might have been less hard for you," she added, with honest pride that she had proved herself to be not unworthy of a portion at least of all this tender solicitude.

Joanna acquiesced sorrowfully. "I was think-ing only of myself when my tongue ran away with me just now," she replied ; "I was thinking that it was worse for me to bear this separation than for you, because you have made yourself everything to me, Ursula. But, after all, that should make it all the sweeter to look back : besides, my pain, however bad it may be, cannot last very long."

"You mustn't talk like that, Aunt Joan," said the girl, caressing her, "or you will make me show you how thoroughly unpleasant I can make myself with very little trying. Why, don't you know how often we fall out over all sorts of things ? There was only the other day when I made you quite cross with me about—"

"There, there," interrupted the other almost smiling, "I don't want to be told all the times I have behaved like an obstinate old woman, my dear. I know I shall always be getting into Hilda's bad books without you to help me keep out of 'em," and she rubbed her nose with an antici-patory air of annoyance at the increase of sisterly friction that promised to be one result of her coming bereavement.

"Ah, but you'll be deprived of one of your chief bones of contention, you see, so that will make some difference."

"What a wicked girl you are, Ursula, to try

and provoke me like this! I declare I shall be finding fault with you soon."

Then they both laughed rather sadly, — a dangerous experiment, which threatened very soon to react powerfully on certain glands known as lachrymal. However, they managed to stop in time, and set to work making plans for the future.

" For you mustn't suppose that I've done with you yet by any means, Aunt Joan," said Ursula ; " you will have to set apart a great deal more of your time for correspondence than you do now. I shall want your advice about everything, just as I always have done, you know,—more, I shall need it more, because—"

She faltered, and stopped.

" Yes, dearest, all I can do you shall have ; a word will bring me to your side. You will not be uncared for, depend upon it. There are— there will be others—" Joanna was labouring to say something about expressing which she apparently found a difficulty,—" others to watch over you, and be close at hand, when you seem to be alone. I mean, we never know who may not come forward unexpectedly to help us," she concluded somewhat lamely.

" Yes, it would be hard if I could not make a few friends of some kind or another in London," mused the girl absently. " I wonder whether I shall be able to keep up drawing and music," she went on; "but my work—for I shall have to earn something—will not leave time for much more than housekeeping, I'm afraid. Ah, that is the worst part: he will never let me improve myself in my own way, and I shall remain as ignorant as I am now of half the riches in the world."

Joanna sighed: "You must try to get your own way in that; you may find your father more tractable than you think:" but her manner was less reassuring than her words. There was, indeed, no colourable pretext for crediting Mr. Lorton with the least vestige of surreptitious amiability.

"Do you remember the legend we heard in the caves at Marchland, Aunt Joan? It may be superstitious, but I cannot help feeling as if we ought to have listened to it as a warning of what was going to happen."

The thought was no new one to Joanna: it had occurred to her even while the tale was being told, heightening her anxiety for her charge's future. Nor, as it turned out, had her fears been groundless. The actual fate reserved for Ursula seemed scarcely less desperate than that which overtook the hapless renegade of the story.

There was a distant general resemblance between the two cases, Aunt Joan admitted.

"Oh, more than that," cried Ursula; "the likeness is quite curious when you come to think of it. This ring now, doesn't it remind you of the poor boy's amulet?" and she held up her left hand till the light fell full on the gem, making it flash again.

"There are no initials on the stone," she went on, "but there's a motto engraved inside; look."

She took it off, first removing the guard, and handed it to Joanna.

"*Amor rex et lex;* and yet Love cannot always hold its throne against disloyalty, Ursula," said she; "what if it is forced to abdicate in your case too?"

The girl put the ring back on her finger before replying. Then she made answer bravely:

"I am enrolled now, dear, and mean to fight hard for the royalist cause."

A tear glistened for an instant on her bright head as she spoke, and lost itself among the soft meshes that twined loosely in a gracious coronet for the tender, dauntless brow. Ursula did not notice it; she only felt that Aunt Joan had leaned quietly back in her chair. There was a pause, during which Joanna tried vainly to torture her features into an expression of sternness. Giving up the attempt at last, she protested that women were hardly-used creatures in being burdened with so much more than their fair share of fortitude.

"If we were not so long-suffering, my dear, men would have to be less selfish, and life would be a more comfortable thing than it is."

Miss Blunsden, mature innocent! was entirely unconscious as yet that anything of an unusual nature had been going on under her roof during the last few days. She could not be kept in ignorance any longer, however, and Aunt Joan took upon herself the thankless task of breaking the news to her sister. That good woman took it with exemplary resignation. She even bore up with such amazing cheerfulness that an itching desire to give her a good shaking, by which Joanna was grievously assailed, must have proceeded from pangs of jealousy at the sense of her own inferiority. Then Ursula was called into the room, and Aunt Hilda submitted to be kissed by her, never once relaxing her saintly imperturbability.

"We can none of us travel through this hard, weary world without bearing our crosses," she murmured, giving a sigh of relief as she was left alone to settle herself luxuriously in her chair.

"Only somehow one doesn't mind the journey so much when it can be done in a well-hung Pullman Car," observed Joanna in gruff parenthesis; "it's the third-class folks who feel it most."

"But you will be happy in your allotted sphere, child," pursued the Mother Superior in the fervent strain which had gained her such pious distinction among the members of her Guild; "you will be happy if you do not fail in your duty to the Church of your fathers."

Supposing all the girl's ancestors to have been of the same type as her surviving parent, the responsibilities involved in this proviso would not have appeared overwhelming.

Ursula threw herself on her knees at the lecturer's side, much to that virtuous female's discomposure.

"Oh, Aunt Hilda," she cried passionately, "you are not glad to get rid of me, are you?"

Now Miss Blunsden was not proud; oh dear no, it would be quite a mistake to suppose that: still, she was not without a very proper and dignified feeling of self-respect, and that feeling conceived itself to be wounded by Ursula's thoughtless behaviour. Really it was too unbecoming in her to ask such questions.

The woman gave place to the school-mistress. "My dear, you forget yourself strangely," she said in a tone of injured surprise; "we shall miss you very much, 1 am sure," she added reprovingly.

But Joanna drew Ursula away and comforted her, bidding her not to mind Miss Hilda's coldness; it was her way, she had always been so, and could not be different.

"She doesn't mean anything unkind by it; but she might just as well be stretched out on a frame herself, she can think of nothing but her everlasting embroidery."

Meanwhile the victim of this misrepresentation, relieved from her momentary embarrassment, sat purring on about the gay life Ursula was going to lead in town,—gay as measured by her peculiar ecclesiastical standard, that is; for nothing would induce the good lady to reflect that anyone — even Mr. Lorton, whose antecedents seemed to have escaped her memory— could hold opinions widely different from her own in that all-important respect. She enquired after his health from his daughter, begged her to assure him that she was disappointed beyond measure not to have seen him when he called, and desired that she might have timely information of his next visit to Burnport.

So the days wore away,—sadly indeed, but without gloom. For to Joanna and Ursula the sadness was tempered with a joy that no man could take from them, Love's radiance casting its broad shadow of contempt upon all else of minor consequence.

Arnold was remembered, though neither spoke of him to the other. Joanna despatched an urgent appeal to him to return at once, telling him of the crisis, and how powerless they were to meet it. Post after post came in, but no answer rewarded her faithful expectation. She waited, and waiting strove to nerve herself for the worst.

# CHAPTER IX.

## CONTRA MUNDUM.

"Oh human souls, while Time yet rolls,
  Your labours past or scarce begun :
High thoughts, sweet words, the smiles, the tears—
In these ye live through endless years ;
  I move in your midst, and we are one.

"Oh my heart's Love, all maids above,
  My life's pure light, my soul's sweet sun,
Dear, you are all the world to me ;
One kiss, and griefs and fears must flee,
  And You and I in God grow one !"—*Loose Leaflets.*

"WELL, Robur, you have seen a good many things since last we met; do you find that your enlarged experience has tended to settle your convictions ?"

The speaker was a man of middle age, with something of that peculiar air which long residence in either university is wont to bestow; anyone skilled in the ways of men would have put him down as a don without hesitation. He was slight, and somewhat delicate-looking; but the full jaw and firm lips, with a humorous smile flickering about the corners, showed that he was anything but a weak man; while his face, which might otherwise have seemed somewhat cold, was made singularly attractive by a pair of very kindly grey eyes. Arnold had left London with his brain in a state of wilder chaos than ever after Paston's disclosures, and betaken himself to the shades of his Alma Mater: and had gladly accepted an invitation to spend the Sunday evening which was to be his last at Cambridge in the company of his former coach at St. Boniface's. Arnold was a Trinity man himself; but circumstances had brought him into connexion with this man, who was popularly known among a certain circle of more or less ardent disciples as Sokratidion. The casual acquaintance had ripened in a rather unusual way into a strong friendship, and our hero was one of the most uncompromising worshippers of the sage of St. Boniface's, in whose rooms they were now sitting together, discussing the philosophic pipe.

Arnold sat gazing at the fire some moments before he answered.

"No, it hasn't," he said presently. "When I went down I fancied that I had got a tolerably clear theory of life of an optimistic character. But my theory was inadequate; it is foggy; like the Cheshire cat, it is fading away with a grin on its face—and the optimism is going with it." ·

"Inadequate—yes. It is no easy matter to deduce a universe from a shell picked up on the sand : the next pebble we see may upset all our theory."

"No doubt," said Arnold : "at four-and-twenty one's knowledge is limited enough. But in the years that have passed over men's heads since John the Baptist was preaching in the wilderness, we might have found something to go on." He spoke drearily, almost angrily.

"We found a good deal to go on, even before that," answered the other, "and a good deal since. I fear your experiences have not been wholly pleasant. How long is it since we learned that the earth goes round the sun ? Men were told pretty constantly for several centuries that physical science was presumptuous and empty enquiry into the hidden things of God ; but we have exploded that notion. Surely we are not going to give in to the same theory about the other fields of knowledge."

Arnold was in a desperate mood.

"To what end ? " he replied. "At twenty we have picked up a shell or two ; at fifty a few more ; at seventy we have a small heap ; and just as we feel that we are beginning to be ready to begin—the candle goes out. 'Man goeth forth to his work and to his labour until the evening.' Yes—and then ?"

"And then it is all over, you would say. But—is it?"

Robur looked up. "Why not?" he said; "and if not, will that help me? I don't want to spend eternity rolling a stone up-hill, and being rolled down again by it. I have no ambition to emulate Sisyphus in another world though I seem to follow his example pretty consistently in this one. It would be worse than orthodox fire and brimstone."

"Is that the only alternative, Robur? I am not going to offer you the hope, held out in most of our pulpits, of the resurrection of the body—which is not saved from bearing to the masses a purely materialistic import by such phrases as a 'spiritual body,' which to most people is merely unintelligible; nor am I going, on the other hand, to deny what is quite a different affair, the perpetuity of individual consciousness. But I don't mean to lay stress on it either by asking, 'Is it all over?' That question is not necessary for our present discussion."

"How do you mean?" said Arnold, relighting his pipe, which he had allowed to go out. "My personal continuance doesn't affect the question of its being all over?"

"Look out of the window, Robur," said the other.

Arnold complied, knowing his friend's eccentric methods of illustration. "By Jove," he said, "it's a splendid night. The moon is glorious. But what's the point?"

"What about the sun?"

Arnold was puzzled. "The sun?" he said, interrogatively.

The man they called "Sokratidion" smiled. "Yes," he said: "the sun. He set hours ago, you say; but the moon is shining with his light for all that. Plato died and was buried two thousand years ago; but we live by his light now as much as men did then. How much of our modern thought is directly due to him? Is it all over with Plato, or Paul of Tarsus? Don't talk to me of death, my friend. Dust to dust is true of kings and philosophers and poets, but it is no mere metaphor to say they never die. The *Iliad* and the *Odyssey* may have been written by one hand, or a hundred; however that be, Homer lives to-day. Shakespeare lives as truly and fully as when he married Anne Hathaway."

Arnold sat down again, but made no reply.

"This seems to be undeniable, Robur: yet it is overlooked, unaccountably enough, in the current dogma of Christianity. By 'eternal life' we are taught to understand continued consciousness: though it is curious that no preacher will precisely treat eternal death as the cessation of consciousness—though I suspect that the perpetual enforcement of the notion of eternal life so conceived as desirable is partly responsible for the popular fear of death. Of course it is an illogical piece of confusion; but I think it is a fact. It can hardly be argued that man necessarily in the nature of things longs for this kind of immortality. I once read of a little girl to whom the nature of future life was so explained; and her teacher was horrified by the answer. 'What,' she said, 'will it go on for ever—and ever—and ever?' 'Yes, my dear; for ever, and ever, and ever.' 'Oh! . . . . It makes me feel so tired!'"

Robur laughed. "I can understand it," he said.

"The feeling is not specially rare, I fancy. But the doctrine is in part also responsible for the materialistic conceptions of the orthodox masses—outside of whose ranks, by the way, I have rarely met a real materialist. To them there is nothing of metaphor in the talk of heaven and hell. They think of them as real *places;* they expect—themselves—to go to the former, and sit on golden thrones singing 'Hallelujah' to all eternity, while their brothers and sisters baste in the bottomless pit. And you may almost lay it down that the more vulgarly material their conceptions are, the more certain they feel of their own salvation."

"I fully agree with you," said Arnold, "and I can't help thinking that there is a good deal of justification for a remark that was quoted a good deal when I was up."

"What was that?"

"One an undergrad. made; it strikes me as being rather to the point. 'For climate,' he said, 'give me Heaven; but for society ——.'"

Sokratidion's eyes twinkled. "Yes," he said, "and it is precisely the view of things which makes such a remark possible that I am attacking. With a loveless heaven, and all the noblest souls in Gehenna, I should prefer the brimstone lake as a question of superior happiness. It is the outcome of our habit of insisting on one view of immortality which may be true, to the exclusion of another which is certainly true. I don't deny personal immortality; it is not inconsistent with the other; but it is on the other that we have to lay stress, now at any rate."

"I see something of what you mean," said Arnold, "when you say that Shakespeare or Plato are still living; or the dozen authors of the *Iliad*, if there were a dozen, though their names are lost, and we swallow them all up in Homer. But I hardly see how that affects the mass of mankind, who go down to their graves and leave no '*monumentum aere perennius.*' The men who have wrought mighty works may live, though their names perish : but we who do no mighty works, we ordinary landlords, shop-keepers, undistinguished privates in the great army—it seems to me that we are the merest ephemerae."

"Who told you that the ephemerae perish ? If a midge dines off you, its little existence may be terminated by severe indigestion, or the simple process of a slap on the back : but you will go home ; possibly, man being frail, you will stamp when the bite twitches : your heel descends on somebody's toe, and in an access of passion he brains you with the poker, for which the law very properly will hang him ; he being a youthful poet, his premature end will bring his works, which ought to have perished, into notoriety, and he will live for ever. All due to that ephemerae you spoke of so slightingly just now. It is the midge that lives for ever : don't speak rudely of midges."

Arnold laughed again. "Admitting the possibility of our diminutive friend's—or enemy's—immortality, if the programme you sketch is carried out, that is practically giving him his monument outlasting bronze. What if I *don't* tread on the budding poet's toe ? "

"Kindly look out of the window again."

" Well, what is your parable now ? "

" How many stars do you see ? "

" How many ? say ten millions; I'm not an astronomer."

" And how many are there you don't see ? "

" $X^n$, I should think," said Robur: "now expound."

" My friend," said the philosopher, " if one solitary star out of all those millions had been omitted by the Creator, the whole arrangement of the universe would have been altered. Say it is a star so far off that it will take another twenty million years for its light to reach us— no matter, the whole system would have been affected by its non-appearance. There is nothing so small, so seemingly unimportant, that we can afford to say 'It makes no difference.' No flower that ever blossomed wastes its sweetness on the desert air. The seed has influenced the history of the universe. That pestilential visitant of sea-side 'lodgings with an ample sea-view,' the arch enemy of slumber who may only be spoken of periphrastically, so that we must use about a hundred syllables to describe him — more or less—instead of his proper ONE, the parent of many curses, who sets you swearing at your landlady, has had a permanent effect on your character.

" Don't suppose I'm joking, Robur," he went

on after a short pause; "I may express myself
jestingly, but I am talking serious truth for all
that. There is nothing in this world so mean,
so common or unclean, that it will not stand to
us for a symbol of immortality. Every trivial
thought, word, or act has its consequence; con-
tributes its mite towards producing some effect.
If midges and fleas have their immortality, what
shall we say of man? Man more than any other
living being affects the course of the world's
history. You say you understand me when I
claim for Plato, or Alexander, or Hannibal the
same immortality which belongs to the martyr
whose death-cry is a shout of victory, whose
dirge is a pæan of triumph. But I tell you that
Judas Iscariot is immortal too; for good or for
evil, the prophet and the traitor alike do their
work, and live for ever, inasmuch as their work
lives. And not only they, but those too whose
names and deeds are alike forgotten. Men look
on the little mound in the churchyard with its
tiny cross, and wonder at the mystery of a life
ended almost before it was begun; but I say that
the very babe which just struggles into the light
to turn its face to its mother and die, is immortal
with Socrates and Shakespeare. Who shall say
of the mother that she can ever again be as if
that moment had not been? The little one is
laid under the sod—but its work is done; a

chapter in the world's history is written in the
line that marks its burial-place."

The solemn tones of the speaker ceased ; for
some minutes neither of the men uttered a word.
Arnold was the first to break the silence.

" Yes," he said, " that is a fine thought.   It
is an easy enough thing to talk of the tramp of
Cæsar's armaments still resounding through
Europe, or the dagger of Burke still lying on the
floor of the House of Commons : we can all see
that pretty readily.   But we don't often think
of extending the conception as you have done."

" To my mind," said the other, " this consciousness gives an infinite solemnity to life.   On
every choice we make there rests, in however
small a degree, the course of the universe through
eternity.   It sounds like inordinate exaggeration,
but for all that it is true ; there is no cause but
has its effect, fixed and certain : we reject alternative sequences as we reject spontaneity.   The
chain is unbroken.   The present contains the
whole of the future : it contains also the whole
of the past.   So, in another sense than that
which the words ordinarily bear, we may say,
' That which was, is : and that which is, will be :
and there is nothing new under the sun.'   In
another sense, because even while we say it, we
know that all things being one and eternal are
yet constantly moving and changing.   To us the

great sea, always one, never the same, is the fittest emblem of the universe. Physicists tell us, and we hail their words as the counterpart of the doctrine, that the sum of energy is constant, and the sum of matter constant; but only because change also is constant. If you wish to feel the magnitude of the thought in all its intensity, go up into the mountains, or gaze out on the ocean ; fly from the roar of the streets, the rush of society with its mass of petty details, or you will lose your touch of the whole. These things are good in their way, but we must escape them now and then, and take refuge in solitude ; suffer our spirit to feel immensity, and our soul to commune with the Eternal. So our heart knows that our small joys and sorrows are as transitory nothings, save as tiny parts of a mighty whole : they shall perish, but the verities of which they are symbols shall endure, and endure eternally. And they to whom is granted the beatific vision return with new strength and peaceful hearts to the 'trivial round, the common task ;' though their time be passed in nothing more splendid than

> ' That best portion of a good man's life,
> The little, nameless, unremembered acts
> Of kindness and of love.' "

Again there was a pause, while the two men sat and smoked silently. Arnold's mind had gone back to that first walk of his with Ursula.

There was a tinge of bitterness in the thought. Half unconsciously he began blowing rings.

"There," he said with a half-laugh, as he watched the wreaths of smoke eddying round in a particularly successful circle, "there is your emblem of immortality."

"The ring was scattered by your breath, Robur, but your words were true enough for all that; we mustn't forget that change is as needful as constancy. You know the saying of Heraclitus."

"Which might vulgarly be called 'shop.' Well, shop covers most things worth talking about. The word is another bit of Philistinism."

"Philistinism, materialism, vulgarity, whichever of the three you choose; though I won't join in your condemnation of the word, which is useful. But the objection to talking shop is one of the marks of the Philistinism which is the bane of all popular thought and practice—or most of it. I'm in a talking mood to-night, Robur, I warn you. Don't let me bore you."

"You're not likely to bore me," replied Arnold, in a tone which implied absolute confidence.

"Well, I am going to do some more tilting at windmills, as some folks might call it, and take the chance of being ignominiously scattered: because it seems to me that an untold number of lives are blighted, more or less, by materialism in one form or another. I know of nothing in respect of which the mass of minds, practically, are more crudely materialistic than marriage."

" I don't know that there is anything particularly remarkable in that."

" Possibly not : yet there is nothing in which it does more harm. I don't know, either, that the Church is of much assistance to us there. Look at that preliminary homily in the Marriage Service—how does it strike you ? "

Arnold looked up with some surprise. " Well, it indulges in some plain speaking ; but surely you don't object to that ? "

His companion laughed. " Not I," he said : " I often wish we had a little more of it. But I suspect you haven't studied that homily. What is the view of marriage it bears on the surface ? No doubt you can read a great deal into it that would spiritualize it immensely ; but without reading between the lines, what does it say ? In effect this : that marriage is an institution for the purpose of keeping men straight ; for the convenience of society ; and the procreation of children. That is the authoritative announcement of the Prayer-Book ; though of course it is not the teaching of the better men in the Church. Well, is marriage no more than that ? The theory is the natural outcome, in one way, of the mediæval ascetic notions. Love is regarded as a 'carnal desire'; carnal desires are wicked, and there is no good word to be said for them; but, as people *will* marry, we had better put the best face we can on it, and give our sanction in a semi-condemnatory manner. Well, what is the result? Love and marriage being treated as marks of our fallen nature, the whole conception of them is degraded. The views of society run parallel with the doctrine of the Church; and marriage becoming simply a question of convenience, Love is no longer regarded as a necessary preliminary: it is the foolishness of youthful romance."

"And yet novels which don't uphold love, and finish up with a crash of wedding bells, are very little read. Doesn't that militate against your theory of the general contempt for love?"

"Not a bit, my friend," said Sokratidion, rising and taking his stand with his back to the fire: "not a bit. Nobody wants to get rid of youthful romance altogether; it is pleasant for the fancy to dwell on. We like our fairy tales, but we don't believe in fairies. We keep romance going, but we don't want it to interfere in practical life. Try your woman of the world, who reads her poetry and her novels: get her on to one of her favourite bits of washy sentimentality: she will gush over it beautifully: '*so* charming, *so* romantic ; " and then watch her trying to hook young Midas for her eldest darling. I don't know that the marriage market is regulated so entirely by money considerations as it has been ; Thackeray's pen couldn't have been without some effect ; but I don't believe love is much more to the fore than it was. We prefer to veil our Mammon-worship. ' Doän't thou marry for munny, but goä wheer munny is ' is the regular maxim."

" But look at the question practically," said Robur, puffing at his pipe viciously : " which are the happy marriages ? How often are we told that a far larger proportion of love-marriages than of *mariages de convenance* end unhappily ? "

" There are two facts which explain that view of the matter : one, that half the ' love-marriages ' aren't love-marriages at all ; the other is, the nature of ordinary marriages. Why should they be actively unhappy ? People enter on them with very low ideals. The woman gets what she wants—butter to her bread ; the man gets what he wants—a decorative head to his establishment. If they are tolerably sensible people, with an average supply of tact, there need be very little friction."

" Well, is that such a very debased state of things ? "

" I call it so, beyond doubt. It is elevating

to neither husband nor wife; and love and marriage should elevate both."

" Look at the other side of the picture then. What about the love-marriages ? "

" I told you, half of them aren't love-marriages. Two young people get up a little liking for each other, both being agreeable enough; and, as they aren't old enough to have got the romance out of them, they fancy they are in love, and go and marry on nothing a year. They aren't in love a bit : they have only a worked-up, sentimentalised liking for each other. Naturally, they find that out afterwards ; they had some sort of ideality about their notion of what married life would be, and they are all the more disappointed when they find they don't prove much use to each other : so they each think the other to blame, and bicker, and quarrel, and the gulf widens, and the world looks on and says, ' Look what comes of marrying for love ! ' " And the sage began walking up and down the room, apparently in a state of most unphilosophic excitement.

" Look here," he went on, turning in a far corner of the room and facing Robur : " I tell you what it is ; Mrs. Grundy is at the back of it as usual. No doubt the excellent old lady has her merits, and prevents accidents here and there ; but the harm she does outweighs the good infinitely. She successfully prevents the possibility in most cases of a man and woman knowing each other tolerably well before they are married. What can a man, ordinarily, know of a girl? Two or three dances; a few calls; a conversation in the conservatory—and the business is done. The knot is tied; and man and woman are man and wife before they are even friends: then they begin to know a little of one another. There is an astonishing amount of guess-work in these matters. If there wasn't, we should have to adopt the universal *mariage de convenance*, or the Malthusian problems would cease to puzzle us with startling rapidity: we should have to send out to Melbourne and Sydney for colonists to keep the population of England going. But that is by the way. As it is, the moment a man lets a girl a little way below the surface of him, he is supposed to have 'intentions'; that is one of the greatest bars to what I hold as the true ultimate condition of marriage being sanctioned, that the man and the woman should love each other wholly."

" You attack the world pretty warmly on that head: are you going to attack the flesh with the same zeal?"

"The flesh? Yes, if you mean by that the doctrines of sensualism which some people are holding up as the gospel of the nineteenth century, as a curative for Philistinism. That is

the worst blasphemy of all, to my mind. But
I am not going to adopt the position of the
people who want to get rid of the flesh altogether ;
who would say that Love, if it be admitted at all,
must be merely the union of two souls. It is
that on its higher side, no doubt ; but that is
only one aspect of it. ' The value and significance
of flesh ' once learnt ' we can't unlearn ten minutes
afterwards.' No man need be ashamed to tremble
at the touch of a little hand, the glance of a
bright eye, the smile of a red mouth. We want
our loves to be beautiful : it is vanity to talk of
flesh fading. You might as well tell a man that
the everlasting hills will be flattened out, as that
his mistress will some day be ugly. She will be
beautiful to him for all time. Byron's

> 'I know not if I could have borne
> To see thy beauties fade,'

was worthy of the man who never loved in his
life. I don't know if the quotation is correct,
by the way, but he has lines to that effect. If
he had loved, the beauties never could have
faded. People who want to get rid of the
animal in man are doing very little better than
our friends we were talking of just now, who
want to give us resurrected protoplasm in place
of our immortal souls."

"Hullo—take care : it's as well some people

didn't hear that. You would be hooted as a blasphemer."

" Why ? " said the other, laughing, " for calling flesh protoplasm ? The resurrection of protoplasm is what half our friends believe in. Saint Paul never said it ; but if it is what they believe, why is it blasphemy to say so ? If it isn't, if nobody believes in it, so much the better ; but where is the blasphemy ? "

" Never mind. Logic is useless in these cases. Go on."

" Well," said the other, returning to his chair, and sitting down again, " I don't know that we need say much about these people, except by way of showing that we aren't theorising without a due regard to the facts of life. The thing I want to arrive at is this : that Love, instead of being shoved aside and looked upon as a light matter, a feeling easily stirred and easily got rid of again, should hold its true place as the noblest and most purifying power in a man's life. Plenty of people agree in that theory ; there is no novelty about it ; but they don't agree in practice : and the actual belief in loving once and for ever is wofully rare. And the reason is partly that folks won't distinguish between liking and loving ; " and he turned to put some fresh coal on the fire.

" But what is one to do ? " said Robur. " You

say yourself that it is a hard matter for a man to get rational ground for loving a girl; mostly, we only get the chance of doing what you would call, I suppose, taking a fancy to her."

" Yes. I don't say the road is an easy one to travel. A man has to think what he is about; his 'fancy' must be an uncommonly strong one. Somehow, most men of at all imaginative natures can make an angel out of very small materials, though. A very strong fancy indeed may be the outcome of a very slight acquaintance : and such a one may, I should say, be pretty well relied on. But it must be capable of surviving a tolerably long separation. If it does that, I should say it has grown to be Love—and a man may well stake his life on the chance. Love is no mere liking : it is a worship; it takes a man out of himself and brings him into communion with Eternity : it is a perpetuation of that beatific vision of which I spoke just now : to know it is worth any conceivable risk. It makes a man ready not merely to die for his beloved,—that is an easy matter,—but to live for her : to live for her, if it must be so, without reward even. ' 'Tis better to have loved and lost '—the saying is sometimes made a subject of college debating societies. What do they know about it ? No one who knows what Love means can question it."

" I don't know," said Arnold mournfully.

" You don't ?   Ask yourself again whether it
is true two years hence.   You will know then."

Arnold saw that he had let out his secret :
he looked up at his companion.

" My friend," said the other quietly, " I know
you well enough to say what your answer will
be.   You will know that you were elevated by
the feeling : you will know that its fruit is not
dead in you : you will recognise the truth of what
I have said, and am going to say.   From your tone
I should say—forgive me if I am wrong—that
you have not lost yet, but fear that you have."

Arnold was silent.

" Well then, come what will, I should tell you
to hold to your love.   It is a bitter thing to know
that the woman one loves has given her heart to
another ; but it is better even so to endure silently
than to lose your hold.   At any rate, remember
this : it is no real love which will not trust too.
Trust her heart—there may be matter you know
nothing of.   Trust her heart, even if you know
that her judgment has led her astray.   And if
hope still remains, bear this in mind—that there
is nothing in this world worth the winning in
comparison with a true woman's love.   Fame is
a pleasant thing ; it is good to have your laurels ;
but the winning them gives no joy like the laying
them down at the feet of one woman.   Would
any true lover change places with a Napoleon, a

Goethe, a Rubens ? Statesmen, soldiers, poets, and painters,

> ' Shut them in
> With their triumphs and their glories and the rest.
> Love is best.' "

Again there was a long pause. Arnold was gazing into the fire ; his companion went to the window and stood watching the twinkling stars.

Arnold started, and looked at his watch.

" Do you know the time ? " he said ; " I must be off, I'm afraid. I have to catch an early train in the morning."

" Well then, we must say good-bye, I suppose," said the other, returning from the window.

" I'm afraid so. By the way," said Robur, laughingly, " some of our friends would have been surprised to hear you to-night, if they looked on you—as I did—as a confirmed bachelor."

His companion looked at him and hesitated a moment before answering. " Yes. You and I are friends, Robur. Look here."

He went to a corner of the room and unlocked a desk. Out of it he took a small packet, and gave it to Arnold.

Arnold unfolded the paper and looked. Just a lock of hair, and a date : that was all. Reverently he folded it again, and returned it silently; and the two men shook hands, and parted without another word.

# CHAPTER X.

## PENITENTS.

*" The sweets of love are washed with tears."—Carew.*

" I'm blest if I can make head or tail of it," observed Mr. Gibbins, partly to himself and partly for the behoof of Mrs. Marchpane and Rhoda, who were engaged in making Arnold's library uncomfortably clean and orderly. " 'Ere hev he bin a-droppin' in three days runnin' ; and when I says the master ain't come back, and waits for him to leave a message or suthink, it's just ' Thankye, maybe I'll look in again to-morrer,' and orf he goes. I never knowed anyone pay his attentions so reg'lar afore." Thereupon Gibbins scratched his head, and contemplated the house-keeper in an aggrieved fashion.

" Well, I never ! " was that cosy matron's elliptical rejoinder ; " you don't mean to say that was Mr. Frank you were talking to just now, Joshua ? I dare say now you frightened him speaking so short and peppery."

The bailiff felt flattered by this gratuitous compliment to his power of striking awe into a fellow-creature.

"Comes prancin' up without a coat, and a snow-storm just beginnin'," he went on, commenting severely on the visitor's injudicious disregard of his personal welfare: "axed him if he'd like the carriage umbrella to keep him from gettin' soaked, thinkin' as it wouldn't matter lendin' it just for the day, yer see; but not he. I don't b'lieve in a man a-physickin' of hisself, bein' what yer may call tenacious o' quacks, as a gen'ral rool, myself; but I specks they'll hev to call in the doctor to him if he goes on like this."

"My certies!" exclaimed Mrs. Marchpane, allowing her attention to wander from the wonderful remarks of the philosopher in leggings to the flakes which were already falling sparsely outside: "Open the window quick, Rhoda, and let's get rid of this dust before the snow gets worse."

Here was a piece of imprudence not to be countenanced by the cautious Gibbins.

"You'll both catch your deaths of cold," he remonstrated; "winders ain't meant to be opened where there's human beings about, leastways not on a day like this, an' no fire neither. Seems to me as most aliments is doo to draught. Ah, you

needn't look s'prised, mum; there's Scriptur
warrant for it. I dunno where I heard it—in
a sermon, prob'ly—but the fust winders was
them as Noah putt in the Ark, an', sure enough,
ages went down uncommon sharp arter that."

This masterly specimen of exegesis was too
much for Rhoda; she was fain to hold her sides
before she could unbolt the sash. Mrs. Marchpane going to her assistance, happened to glance
through the pane, and gave a little start.

" Why, if that isn't the Burfield cab coming
up the drive," she said.

" Right you are, mum," was Joshua's confirmation, as he peered over her at the very unmistakable vehicle in question; " and Mr. Arnold's
portmanty on the top," he added, smiting his leg
with something as nearly approaching gleefulness
as it was possible for him to exhibit.

They all hurried to the door just as they were
to receive our hero, who was accompanied by
Frank Dalton. That young gentleman had met
Arnold upon the road, and been asked to take
his seat in the cab.

" A precious good thing, too, for you, sir; else
you'd have bin turned into a walkin' hicicle, rest
upon me," asseverated Gibbins, in an aside
designed for his private ear.

The short interval which Arnold had spent at
Cambridge had done him a great deal of good.

He felt clear now on some points which were obscure enough before. If all things do *not* come to an end, as modern science seems to affirm, at least doubt and harrowing uncertainty are among those that do.

He had tried hard to persuade himself that he must get over his passion; but he had failed, and then for a while his mind had been thrown into a state of turmoil. The relief afforded by breathing a purer atmosphere of thought had changed all this: he saw plainly for the first time, not merely that he was too deep in love to draw back, but that he had been wrong to think of drawing back. His heart was right after all, and he must somehow have gone astray over that notion about Frank. Appearances had certainly been against the boy, but he had been too hasty in believing them for more than they were worth. No, no; Frank had not supplanted him, and all the rest was easily forgiven. He was half inclined to jump out and tender an apology to Frank for his groundless suspicions when he met that promising youth toiling home against the wind. All he did, however, was to answer the other's stare of surprise by shouting to the driver to stop, whereupon his young friend came sheepishly up, and took Arnold's proffered hand.

He seemed a trifle less dull and heavy for

all his awkwardness, though : perchance some goddess had taken pity on her clownish worshipper, and wrought this metamorphosis in him in her unwillingness to accept the homage of any graceless thing. Yes, that must be it ; but was this long-suffering condescension the same thing as the goddess' unconditional surrender of herself to one chosen out from all her followers ? Supreme love for that one could not limit her natural care for the rest.

" Come back with me," said Arnold kindly, opening that one particular door in the Burfield cab which could under any circumstances be induced to act *as* a door, and not as a permanent fixture solely designed by the philanthropic builder for the free circulation of draught, dust, and mud in minute quantities inside the vehicle.

Frank complied with the invitation, and no sooner did they jolt onwards than he began to pour out disjointedly the plea for forgiveness which his long delay had made so difficult.

The roar of the wind combined with the rattling and creaking of the cab to form an accompaniment so loud that it almost drowned his words. This probably accounted for Frank's incoherent volubility ; for after he had once managed to unclose his lips there was no dearth of material to bring him to an early close ; he had to shout on account of the noise, which was less embarrassing than speaking in the midst of complete silence would have been; you cannot very well falter when you are talking at the top of your voice. Arnold stopped him as soon as he could.

"Stay and clear up the whole business for me," he said as they alighted, having reached the house.

They were soon snugly seated in the dining-room, and secure from interruption Frank told the story of his connexion with the bookseller and the bookseller's colleague, as far as he himself was aware of it. A few carefully put questions elicited the fact that he knew nothing about Ursula's real history, and was quite happy in the supposition that she was an orphan niece of the sisters Blunsden.

There was an honest confusion about young Dalton's manner whenever her name was mentioned that convinced Arnold still more strongly of the truth of his latest impressions, making him admit that on this point at least the lad had developed feelings which deserved respect.

It was after some clumsy revelation of the light in which he regarded Miss Lorton, and the sort of intimacy between them, that Frank added, blushing very red indeed, " I don't know that I should have come here and made a clean breast of it at all, if it hadn't been for her : she put me up to doing it. I suppose there aren't many like her : she talks quite differently to what any-one else does, you know. And it's not all just *talk ;* she takes an interest in one. There's *some-thing* in her—well, I can't explain it, and I don't suppose you would see it if I tried."

Arnold turned aside to put some coals on the fire. Somehow or other he managed to drop a considerable portion of the shovel's contents on to the carpet, and could not reply till he had removed the traces of this misfortune.

"Now, Frank, I'm going to ask you an odd sort of question," he said at last, when the operation was completed. "Did Miss Lorton ever tell you anything about that ring of hers ? There, I won't ask you anything more if you'll answer that."

Frank did not look very much surprised. Normally his character was not emotional, and he had been having such a surfeit of surprises lately that one more or less made very little difference to him.

"Yes ; I asked her once if she could remember anything before she went to live with the Miss Blunsdens, and then she showed me the ring, and said that it had belonged to her mother, but that she knew hardly anything about her. I can't remember much about it, except that she didn't seem to want me to go on, it seemed to bother her ; so I left off."

Then they began to discuss the future. " Try Texas for a time " was Frank's own prescription for himself ; his brother was getting on out there pretty well after a hard struggle, and Mr. Dalton had been hinting the possibility for his remaining son of finding a new hemisphere for his talents also.

Arnold refrained from expressing an opinion. He knew nothing of new countries, he said, or the sort of men who made desirable colonists. He promised, however, to do all in his power to help the other, whichever side of the Atlantic he should choose.

Their colloquy ended, Frank departed, accoutred in an ample weather-proof overall, while his host reflected with satisfaction that he had never been less glad to get rid of him.

Arnold stood for a few moments in front of the warm blaze, rubbing his hands not so much because they were cold as for keen delight at finding how mistaken he had been in his blind, one-sided judgment of his lady. Lorton had given her the ring; Lorton was the writer of that anonymous letter, the accusations in which had all along been incredible to its reader. He had never really believed those lies against her ; —poor child ! What a father for any daughter to have! Truly she needed all the love that others could bestow to make it up to her.

But Mr. Lorton's existence scarcely troubled him just then : if money was all he wanted, money he should have to go away and cease to trouble his daughter's proper guardians farther. Doubtless she herself knew nothing of his importunity or him; Joanna would have kept her from that. But yet she might discover the secret by some untoward accident. Lorton was in London; that was a good sign. For the present Ursula must be free—but for how long would she remain so? The thought checked her lover in his ecstasy. He resolved to go to Burnport the first thing on the next day, excusing his precipitation on the plea of concerting measures with Joanna Blunsden to get her persecutor out of the country.

Throwing off his brooding fit with a laugh, he first yawned, then had a good stretch, and finally sauntered out, his mind infinitely lightened of anxiety, to see if any papers had been left for him on the library table during his absence.

There were several letters; but he only read one, picking it out from the rest after a brief examination of the post-mark. As he read, the hopeful look faded from his countenance, and with a cry of dismay he began to search feverishly for a railway guide. His fingers trembled so that he could scarcely make use of it when found. At last! There was just time to catch a slow train to Copesbury, where, with the usual admirable arrangement, he would have to wait an hour before the Burnport Express arrived. He must go at once ; to-morrow would be too late. Oh that he had known of the letter sooner ! Even now he might miss getting to his destination that night.

Had not Gibbins been one among a thousand, or had not the railway traffic been hindered by the snow to some extent, these dismal forebodings might have been fulfilled. That experienced retainer's behaviour on the present occasion, however, amply justified the motto which history, so long as his fame endures, will couple with his name. Convinced that his credit as one who in every emergency might be " rested upon " was at stake, he was no sooner aware of the nature of the assistance required of him than, plunging forth bareheaded into the rough scrimmage of the elements, he charged recklessly across the stable-yard, dragged the groom from a pile of hay where he was reposing, shouted to him to harness the black cob in the fraction of a trice, and got the gig out of the coach-house with his own hands. Then he shot back again into the house, bawled out to Mrs. Marchpane to have the master's bag ready, and provided with necessaries, seized his coat, hat, gloves, and whip—all which paraphernalia formed part of the severely useful furniture of his secluded cell—and emerged upon the hall in time to open the door as the gig made its appearance, the sedateness of his demeanour disposing at once of the least suspicion in the minds of others that he had been in any particular bustle.

He even went so far as to remark, in the minute which passed before Arnold came out:

"The way that 'ere 'arness is putt on looks to me downright slov'nly: I tell you what it is, young shaver, you've bin a-hurryin' over it shameful."

The boy at the horse's head protested his innocence, but with no effect except to convert his patron's displeasure into a general prognostication of woe for the entire generation of boys to which this particular individual belonged.

"Talk o' cheek!" observed the bailiff, mildly indignant that his subordinate should have offered to defend himself; "why, in my young days we didn't know what the word meant."

This was strictly true,—almost too strictly, perhaps; for if folks of the earlier generation thus alluded to were ignorant of the word, they knew the thing well enough to evince no mean aptitude for its practical application.

"Cheek what don't blush to conterradict one straight to one's face can't 'spect to enjoy the

priv'leges of a free country, leastways not in a
menial it can't. If you must cheek someone,
cheek your ekals,—or your inferiors, if you've
got any. The more lower down you are the
more people you've got to mind not to cheek.
But there, you ain't fit for a free country, you
ain't; what you want is 'Merican indepenunce.
You'll have to emmygrate to 'Merica, my fine
feller, 'cos nobody ain't nobody's better over
there ; ev'rybody being worse off than ev'rybody
else, and patteronising of each other all round,
like. Waitin' for you, sir," and Gibbins got into
his seat, holding the apron open for Arnold.

They set out in the teeth of the gale, the snow
making their faces smart, in spite of Arnold's
desperate efforts to frustrate it with a monstrous
erection of gingham and whalebone. Manœuvring this parachute so as to prevent the wind from
getting round its corners, in which case it would
have probably involved them in its wreck, was
an occupation sufficient to absorb the whole of
any man's attention for a three-mile drive.
Arnold's arms ached as much as if he had been
dangling at the fag end of a balloon for the last
half-hour when they reached the station-yard at
Burfield, and he tumbled down from his perch,
hot and exhausted.

He hardly knew how they had managed to get
there at all: the cob had settled down to his

work gallantly, though it was plain by the way
in which he shook his ears that the job was as
little to his equine taste as it would have been to
that of any animated creature but a hedgehog.
Gibbins disdainfully declined to see any merit in
his own performance, averring that he could have
done it blindfold. He knocked off with the butt-
end of his whip the white breast-plate encrusted
on his coat, turned on his homeward journey, and
with the wind well in his back was soon lost to
view.

Trains were late and stoppages frequent on
the line, the consequence being that it was too
late when Arnold arrived at Burnport for him
to call on Miss Joanna before the next morning.

A sleepless night followed. He rose and
dressed himself by candle-light, descending to
the cold, deserted coffee-room to find a draggled
chamber-maid going to sleep over an abortive
attempt to light the fire.

Not without considerable difficulty he hired
a messenger to go to East Rise bearing a note to
inform Joanna of his arrival, and begging her to
be ready for him shortly before nine. He returned
to the coffee-room and tried to take some breakfast, but it was useless ; a strip of leathery toast
and half a cup of over-drawn tea was all he could
manage. There was a good deal of time to be
got through before he could start. The messenger

returned with the verbal intelligence that it was
"all right," and he supposed it to mean that he
was expected at the time mentioned. He went
to the reading-room, and sat there with his
watch in his hand. Its hands seemed to stand
still, and every now and then he held it to his
ear to persuade himself that this was not actually
the fact.

At first the intervals at which he did so were
very short; then they grew longer—longer, till
he roused himself from a dreamy stupor to find
that he had already overstayed his time by some
minutes.

A blank,—and he was holding Joanna's hand,
and looking into her eyes.

"Aunt Joan."

"Arnold."

So they stood, neither of them speaking for a
moment.

"It is the eleventh hour, and we can do
nothing — absolutely nothing but share our
sorrow. I never gave you up: thank God
you have come at last."

Tears were in her eyes; but they were not
tears of bitterness; she dried them, smiling
calmly.

Patient soul! there are many more in the
world like yours, fashioned by suffering after the
same great Model. Many who every day and

all day long are living but to conform to that standard, to be counted as sheep for the slaughter; and to whom, when they are looking for nothing in return—not even that reward of other-worldliness on which some would fain busy themselves —joy comes cleaving through the heavens in answer to their faith, scattering sorrow with a gladness all the sweeter because it is so late.

But a numbing paralysis seemed to be creeping over the companion by her side; his hair stirred upon his head, as though some ghostly breath were passing over it; there was a chilling dampness on his brow; his very heart grew faint, and slackened its beat under his panic torpor. Was this horrible fatalism really true after all, then? Nothing to be gained for good by fighting: nothing to be done but submit to evil? Not so: it was indeed the eleventh hour; but what of that? Was love to return empty, robbed of its spoils because so far it had not taken them? They should see.

"Let me explain why I left you," he cried thickly; "have we time?"

There was plenty, Joanna said; so they sat down, and he recounted to her as concisely as he could the history of the ring, tracing it from the time when his mother, warned of her approaching death, placed it in its secret receptacle to its reappearance on Ursula's finger, and concluding

with a sketch of his movements since leaving
Burnport, sufficient to account for his delay in
replying to Joanna's letter.

His friend was much perturbed by this fresh
evidence of Lorton's ingrained villainy. "The
poor child must be told before she goes," said
she, half rising as though to carry out her words
forthwith.

He motioned her back quietly.

"No," he replied with gentle determination;
"it is the only condition I make, and I entreat
you to observe it: when she learns the truth,
let it be from me."

"But is she to go on innocently conniving at
her father's crime?"

"Why not? It cannot matter so long as she
is not made to share his guilt."

Joanna knit her brows thoughtfully.

"No," she returned, yielding that point but
advancing another, "it hasn't done any harm for
her to have it up to now, that is quite true; but
would it be honourable to let her keep anything
which symbolises to others a mutual understanding between you before that understanding
exists?"

"My answer is the same as it was to your
other objection," he pleaded; "whatever her
possession of the ring symbolises now it symbol-
ised before."

"Ah, but your misunderstanding made things seem more complicated then : you thought that there were circumstances which obliged you to hold your tongue, and so you were right in doing so."

"Well, are there no such circumstances still ? Were I to see her now in order to add to her grief, how could I avoid telling her the whole truth,—not merely a trivial fraction of it ? An unchivalrous way of taking advantage of her forlorn situation."

He spoke vehemently. Joanna followed her inclination to trust him, and began to waver.

"She must not be disturbed now by anyone, or she will break down altogether ; and I quite understand that it will be better for you to tell her than for anyone else. And yet suppose her father opens her eyes : he has no reason to dread the consequences, as far as I can see. There are no bounds to his refined brutality. What are we to do?" Clasping her hands the speaker lapsed into silence. Had her brain been ever so fertile of expedients it could scarcely have made satisfactory provision for all the contingencies which beset this problem.

Strenuously controlling his ideas Arnold considered the state of affairs : Ursula upon the point of leaving all that she held dear,—or, at least, that held her dear,—her mind intent upon

but one single aim, the duty of ministering to
her miserable father; that father utterly callous
to his daughter's suffering,—perhaps even enjoying it, if Aunt Joan's opinion of him was
correct,—and ready to turn the ring with reck-
less impunity to any profitable account; the
wrong of shaking Ursula's determination or
needlessly grieving her spirit by fresh disclosures; the equal wrong, as it seemed, of
letting the moment slip when these disclosures,
or one of them, might be most tenderly made;
of giving the maiden up without a word of
comfort, without a hint of warning, to all the
unutterable torture which a ruffian such as
Lorton was sure to inflict; the agonising impossibility of obtruding himself upon her at this
crisis; the no less painful certainty that she
would misconstrue his absence if he allowed
anyone else—even Aunt Joan—to break to her
the contemptible fact of her father's deliberate
insult to her modesty.

This last was the most honourable course to
take, however: he took it, bitterly recalling
Paston's prophetic caution against moral suicide.

"It is no use," he thought, "I cannot help
myself."

"You must tell her," he said presently, addressing Joanna; "she could have no gentler
ambassador to announce misfortune than the

only being in the world who is worthy of her love."

His lips trembled as he closed them, but his look was fixed steadily on the woman before him.

The face with its deathly pallor, the dinted nostrils, the filming eyes, all betokened so terribly the man's starvation for lack of love that Joanna's mind was made up in an instant : she refused point blank to act upon his suggestion.

" No," she said decisively ; " better to take the chance of what may happen than do such an injury to you both. Don't you see, you foolish fellow, that it would be just as bad for Ursula as for you if I were to tell her only half the story ? When she gives up the ring it must be into your own hands, that her grief at discovering the truth about it may be at once turned into the joy of rightful ownership. At least, that is supposing——but really it is very annoying having nothing but suppositions to go on."

She paused to blow her nose, and then proceeded :

" Now, you know, I'm thinking entirely and solely of her in all this. As for you, another occasion must be found—soon found, mind— when she can be honourably rescued. The truth must be told her as a whole, not in your precious instalments. Why, it would come out much more like falsehood than truth that way. No," and Aunt Joan tried to make a great show of virtuous indignation ; " I'm not going to say to the poor darling, ' Mr. Robur has come for his property, my love, and would be much obliged if you could find it convenient to part with it before he loses sight of you ;' you needn't think it."

Oh, most inconsistent person ! An impressive warning, truly, to set before this young man of the scandalous double-dealing to be anticipated in encounters with thy sex !

Arnold, however, with the hare-brained impetuosity of youth, took little heed of the way in which his friend had veered round from her original opinion : he clutched eagerly at the new hope which her change gave him, letting everything else go to the winds.

" Thank you," he said, as he leaned forward to take her hand. " But indeed I don't mean to let her out of my sight at all. What is to be their address in London ? "

She gave him a number in an obscure East End street, and he noted it down carefully.

" Remember that their lodgings have been taken in the name of Edwards—Mr. and Miss Edwards. For more than half his life he has been known by that name chiefly."

Arnold made a note of that also, and then rose.

"The mid-day train?" he asked, and receiving an affirmative reply, "I shall go up by it too, keeping out of sight unless there is any need for my interference," he added.

Joanna smiled approvingly.

"God bless you, dear; you will conquer yet."

She followed him to the door, where he turned, with one hand on the handle, to bid her farewell. A passionate impulse came over him : could his dead mother have been much more to him than this woman had made herself? In a moment his lips were pressed to her wrinkled forehead, and his arms round her.

"Be comforted," he said, loosing his hold.

She leaned on a high-backed chair, and folded her hands.

"I will, I will : yes, even to-day, which has been threatening with evil all these years, has its store of happiness in proportion to its pain."

It certainly was a relief to Joanna that her benevolent sister was out of the way. What with the sudden violence of the weather, and her intense mental agitation, Miss Blunsden was suffering from one of her "attacks." She was, like a female Pope, a prisoner in her small Vatican up-stairs. It was a wise precaution on her part; and between her orisons and her bottles of "light medicine" the day promised to pass over her reverend pate with tolerable smoothness.

"Half-past ten," said Aunt Joan, as the clock struck in the little hall; "I shall have a clear hour with my dear child; her luggage has gone up to the station already."

"Something for you," and Arnold handed her a note out of the letter-box.

Joanna opened it hastily, then turned white. Arnold thought she would faint; but she recovered herself.

"Read it," she moaned.

He picked the scrap of paper up from where it had fluttered, and with a beating heart read the single pencilled line which it contained.

"We could not bear the parting, dearest; have taken an earlier train. Ever your own

*U. L.*"

# CHAPTER XI.

## OUTSIDE THE STATION.

" One whose brute-feeling ne'er aspires
Beyond his own more brute desires.
Such tools the tempter ever needs
To do the savagest of deeds.
For them no vision'd terrors daunt,
Their nights no fancied spectres haunt ;
One fear with them, of all most base,
The fear of death,—alone finds place."—*Marmion.*

BIDDING old Time reverse his waning sand-glass for the space of some four-and-twenty hours—a behest which the sullen tyrant must needs obey from such as rule the destinies of men—we divide on wings of ubiquitous fiction the snow-laden air, and settle reluctantly among the belching chimney-pots of Stepney.

The new lodger had taken possession of his apartments. His daughter was expected to arrive from her situation in the country on the following day, and the fond father chafed irritably to think that he should be kept waiting even so short a time before his domestic gloom could be brightened by her companionship. At least, that is what he told the landlady, who carried on a modest business in fuel,—to which, in the summer months, was added ginger-beer, —and liberally retailed the information gratis to all her habitual customers that afternoon along with the more expensive wares which they came to purchase.

How had Mr. Lorton been spending the last few days? A detailed account of his employ-ments during the interval which separates us from our last glimpse of him would be unpleasant, so we take leave to skip it, merely observing in a general way that he had been taking his pleasure like the man of fashion he aspired (with filial assistance) some day to become.

But he had been spending something else besides time. His money, with the exception of some small change—very small change indeed—had all been dissipated by this time: it would not do to forget that. Ursula would soon fill his pockets again, to be sure, and keep them filled; but meanwhile he must live, and she would bring nothing with her, he knew. Young Robur was not hooked yet, curse him. Delay was dangerous: the fish had been nibbling at the bait, and saw what it concealed. But an expert angler was not to be foiled thus: he would examine his tackle to insure himself against accidents.

The illustration was apt enough, but how was Lorton to apply it in his own case? The answer to this question was compressed significantly into the dissyllable, "Paston!"

Yes, there was nothing to be said against it: the doctor must be pumped on the subject of his friend's present state of mind and plans for the future.

The anxious parent did not know where to find his man, but there was no great difficulty in obtaining the use of a directory for that purpose, and in the course of the evening he presented himself before the house in Wimpole Street.

"Snugger than Stepney," he mused while he waited to be admitted; "h'm, yes, I think this neighbourhood would suit me very nicely during the season; must see about it when I've settled the girl."

Perhaps he was a little rash to propose risking a continued residence in England in this way, though his absence had been a long one. Still, living in London had not been attended with any bad consequences to him hitherto, and the instinct which attracted him to any social centre was not nearly so antagonistic to prudence as might have been supposed.

Dr. Paston was at dinner. On being informed of the gentleman's name he sent word that he was free to wait, if he was so disposed.

The visitor was ushered into a sombre ante-room, where a single jet of gas was burning in dismal despair of ever being of the least use alone to anyone to do anything by.

"Doesn't even ask me to join him," thought the visitor moodily; "British hospitality gone the way of most other British monopolies."

Lorton was kept brooding over his cheerless meditations for fully half-an-hour, and was almost frantic when the servant appeared to announce that Mr. Paston had finished dinner, and would be happy to receive him in the next room.

Inwardly fuming, he complied with this formal invitation.

The doctor was lolling comfortably in an arm-chair with his back to the door by which his visitor entered.

"That frame of mind won't last very long," the latter promised himself as he announced his presence by a cough.

"Mr. Edwards?" and Paston wheeled round to face him. "It's an age since we met, isn't it? And how changed you are! Is it care that has dulled your erstwhile glowing cheek, and thinned your flowing locks (you surely used to wear a beard); or to what cause may we attribute these sad ravages?"

"The razor is in great measure responsible for

the last alteration," replied the victim of this sally somewhat testily; "and as to the other which you are good enough to mention, I take it as a piece of complimentary exaggeration on your part to say that I was ever much given to 'glowing'—except, perhaps, in the terms in which I may at one time and another have advertised my clients' productions."

He was annoyed to see that Paston intended to take no notice of their last encounter if he could help it.

"Well, I trust that your natural force in that respect at least remains unabated," remarked the doctor drily. "You have deserted the *Tuba*, I hear; but probably you have found a more lucrative post elsewhere. Why you should honour this house with your presence, however, I don't know. We do our own advertising here, and can't help you on that score. To come to the point, what do you want?" he added bluntly.

Lorton was in a corner; there was no particular harm to be done by telling the truth. Paston might be his most determined enemy; but he was muzzled as effectively as any of them, and could only show his teeth, not use them.

Ursula's father took a chair unbidden, and broke into a grating laugh.

"What do I want?" he repeated, screening the light of the lamp from his face with his

hand, and peering under it at the other; " I want
my rights ; I want my daughter's rights. Where
is your friend Robur ? Does he mean to abscond
and leave us in the lurch—me and my girl ?
Come, Paston, won't you exert your influence to
make him act on the square, and abide by his
pledges ? "

"It's a curious fact," murmured the object of
this touching appeal, "and may strike you as
somewhat wildly irrelevant, Mr. Edwards, but I
am thinking of turning an honest penny in a
quiet way outside my profession. Between ourselves," he went on, closing his eyes, "the
temptation of placing the Criminal Investigation
Department in communication with one whose
disappearance some years ago was universally
deplored is getting too strong to be resisted.
His friends in and out of the Department have
not forgotten him, and are still prepared to pay
down a really handsome sum, without grumbling,
in return for information which may lead to his
capture. Give me your advice, there's a good
creature."

Lorton laughed again,—a little more uneasily
this time. In the mouth of Robur or "the
Blunsden woman" this would have been an idle
threat; but there was less to deter Paston from
meaning what he said.

" These hypothetical cases are always interest-

ing," was the visitor's sneering rejoinder. "I
should think twice before I tried to ruin a man's
life just because he got into bad company a
quarter of a century ago, before he was old
enough to know better."

"Well, I can't work with your hypothesis, at
any rate; so we'll drop ambiguities, as you wish
it." The speaker straightened his back, un-
crossed his legs, and glared at his opponent.
"How about ruining a woman's life—two women's
lives, if not more? Tell me that."

His sudden change to a tone of fierce aggression
took Lorton somewhat aback.

"A groundless charge," he stammered; "you
couldn't substantiate it if you tried. Would
you convict a man unheard on the sole testimony
of a hysterical old maid?"

The doctor started to his feet.

"Look here," he said, "do Miss Joanna
Blunsden the injury of alluding to her again
with those lying lips of yours, and you'll be a
candidate for a casualty ward. Keep a civil
tongue in your head, and I'll give you a fair
hearing."

This was all that the other desired. His foe
was not so formidable, after all. The simplicity
with which he offered our diplomatist full facilities
for executing his mission was positively amusing.
Paston had only to be got to talk, and Robur's

whereabouts, to say nothing of his projects, would soon ooze out.

With a clever assumption of ingenuousness, Lorton proceeded to enlarge upon the cruelty of the suspicions which had already dogged him through life, preventing him, as he solemnly declared, from ever settling down to an honest livelihood.

"You yourself," he whined, "when I come here to-night on my poor girl's errand, accuse me of sacrificing her interest to my own. Under the circumstances you can hardly be surprised that a hungry and penniless man should say rather more than he means."

"Hungry are you?" said Paston, cruelly ignoring the hint; "that's bad: always eat a good dinner; I invariably prescribe it to highly-strung, nervous constitutions like yours. Pray don't give up the pleasures of the table to call on me another time."

He did not altogether believe in his visitor's lugubriousness.

"Hadn't you better go on at once to explain the errand you mentioned?" he enquired gravely, resuming his seat.

"What is the use, if you don't believe anything I say?" complained the other. "However, you would not, as a man of honour, use your knowledge to hurt an innocent girl; so I will

tell you what I mean. Perhaps you're not aware
that she is wearing an engagement-ring which
pledges—virtually pledges—her to your friend,
and him to her?"

He leaned with his elbow upon the table, and
again shaded his eyes for another scrutiny of the
doctor's face.

Paston was troubled, but took care not to
show it. He was determined to serve his friend's
interests to the utmost, though the best way to
accomplish this was not clear to him at present.
Also he was actuated by an intense feeling of
pity and admiration for Ursula and the woman
who had helped so much to make her what she
was.

Therefore he held his peace, bottling his wrathful disgust at having to endure this man's society.
It was purely a matter of policy, he thought, and
secretly longed that the interview might not
terminate without some excuse for applying a
physical argument.

There was a pause during which each was
considering how to get what he wanted out of
the other. Both were equally upon the defensive now; one for his friend, the other for himself. In such cases that man has the advantage
who has broken his fast most recently. Paston
closed his eyes placidly, waiting for the other to
interrupt the deadlock.

Grinding his teeth with suppressed rage the persecuted widower fired a random shot:

"Silence gives assent as well as consent, I suppose. Well, she's coming up to town to-morrow to look for her young man."

It was a mistake. The enemy was not slow to profit by this warning of the tactics which were to be used against him.

"That seems to me a poor move on your part, if you'll excuse my saying so," he rejoined blandly. "Was it wise to throw over young Dalton in such a hurry? Suppose my friend has cooled down, what will you do then?"

He was beginning to see the lie of the land, and thought he would try a little dissimulation on his own account.

Lorton made a gesture of incredulity.

"She's sweet enough on him, and he'll be as keen as ever when he knows that. When a girl comes after a man herself it's rather difficult to get out of the mess, and a landowner can't cut and run like some more independent people, you know."

"Don't get hypothetical again," remonstrated the doctor; "it's confusing to you as well as to me. Forgive me if I am obtuse, but I can't help doubting whether the matter presents itself to the other interested parties in quite the same light as it does to your unprejudiced paternal mind. My friend, for instance, might feel considerably more delicacy about approaching your daughter now that she enjoys your valuable protection than when he used to meet her down at Burnport. He might be even perverse enough to imagine that it was more considerate not to put himself in her way at all in the present tide of her good fortune. He might not persevere in his attentions openly unless she gave him some assurance that they were not humiliating to her in her new position; and do you think she is prepared to give him the encouragement of her own accord?"

"Psha!" scoffed her father, "she is my daughter, my dear sir; she is no fool. And do you fancy I cannot make her amenable to my wishes? Really, doctor,—ha, ha—you must be joking. Is her wearing that ring no encouragement?"

"It hasn't been so yet, and won't be, till you tell her the truth about it." Paston did not in the least comprehend how the ring had come to Ursula, but he saw immediately his remark was out of his mouth that its aim had been reached.

Lorton had counted upon the doctor's complete knowledge of his various achievements. Information had reached him from Mr. Rock that his share in the theft, as well as in the matter of

Frank Dalton, had been discovered; and his brain, heated by the excesses of the last few days, rushed to the conclusion that there was nothing left to conceal. He was not startled, therefore, to hear Paston hint at the way in which he had tricked Joanna Blunsden into receiving stolen property.

"That's just what I mean to do," he replied doggedly; "I'm going to tell her all about it, and then we shall see what she'll do."

"Yes, that is something interesting to look forward to," assented his involuntary entertainer with irritating calmness. "I suppose there is only one thing we may count upon her not doing," he resumed after a moment's apparent cogitation; "she will not be likely ever to look her lover in the face again."

"Oh, she'll come round after a bit, trust her;" and the man assumed a blustering tone. "Women have only got to see that a thing must be done, and they drop their squeamishness fast enough. Screw 'em up to the proper pitch, sir, and they don't mind what they go through. I didn't know her mother for nothing; and she was a good average sample of a self-willed prude, I can tell you."

"It may be as you say, Mr. Lorton; but, to tell you the truth, you don't impress me with the idea that you are any better posted up in

the thoughts and motives of a good woman than
you seem to be in the manners of a gentleman.
Do you know, you remind me amusingly of an
American lady over here on a visit, whom I met
the other day. Her husband had remained at
home at Chicago, and she began talking to me
about his business. 'He's a pork-packer,' she
said, adding innocently for my edification, ' what
you call a *pro-duce merchant* in the old country,
you know.' An odd notion, wasn't it ?" and the
doctor chuckled.

The widower was biting his nails nervously;
he did not despair of triumphing over the difficulties which might be raised by his daughter's
contumacy. But it would take time, and he was
at the end of his resources. Evidently his position was not so secure as it had seemed. Abject
misery was the best guise to adopt, he thought ;
but his dejection was not wholly feigned as he
lifted up his voice in deprecation of the unjust
resentment which his conduct was innocently
causing.

" Every one is set against me," he complained,
" and why ? Is it so very unnatural for a man
to want to see something of his own child when
she has been abducted from his house, and
brought up out of his reach ? Not that I say
anything against the way in which she has been
kept ; it's most kind and charitable, I'm sure.

And perhaps when my home circle was first broken up I didn't feel it as I ought to have done. But that's neither here nor there : I do feel the want of my girl now. It's my one inducement to lead an honest life that you're taking away from me when you refuse to let me have her. Why, she offered to come of her own free will—I can show you her letter; don't say I forced her."

The doctor had risen during this harangue, and was squaring his shoulders against the high chimney-piece, resting one foot on the fender. He gazed down with a cold interest at the creature before him. Possibly his feelings would have been raised to a higher temperature, had the man's venomous breath been extinct, and Paston invited to lecture a class on what was left.

"What a shockingly bad liar you are !" he exclaimed contemptuously; "you are always contradicting yourself. What has your poor child done that you should smirch her fair young life with your loathsome contact ? You would cheerfully see her spirit broken and her health decayed—and even something worse than either, I do not doubt—if you could grind money out of the process. Pity you !—well, yes, I do, though you cannot expect it; for some day you will die, —a thought that never seems to occur to you and such as you. Now I tell you one thing,

your daughter will starve before she will be made
the excuse for asking Robur, or any one else, to
support you. You were a fool not to see that
before you undertook to provide for two mouths
instead of one. Now it is too late : your only
chance of seeing her married, and getting your
freedom again, lies in finding a respectable employment, and trying to make up for some small
part of the mischief you have done."

An idea came into Lorton's head : try a
dramatic situation !

" Help me to do so, doctor," he cried, springing
up, and trying to grasp Paston's hand.

That gentleman, however, promptly made himself inaccessible to this unexpected overture by
putting both his hands in his pockets.

The other fell back slightly, abashed by this
freezing indifference.

Paston eyed him narrowly.

" I thought it would come to that sooner or
later, and it has come later. Well, how much
do you want me to help you with ? " he enquired
with brusque scorn.

The front-door bell rang while Lorton was
considering.

" Oh come, be quick," said the doctor; " I'm
wanted."

Thus pressed, his visitor had no time for
elaborate excuses.

"A fiver would set me straight," he said hesitatingly.

Paston left the room without replying, and the crestfallen mendicant was left alone to ruminate on his folly in not having extorted double the amount.

The man of business reappeared in his coat and hat.

"Now," he observed, extending a clean bank-note to the man of pleasure, "I dare say you may be surprised at my weakness in giving you money. But it's intended for your daughter, not for you. Of course, I am not such an idiot as to think that she will get it. No matter; I can do no more, and I'm not going to do less. If you spend it all upon yourself, the blame be upon your head : perhaps some driblet of it may reach her. Anyhow, remember this ; if you ever want any more from me, you must bring me satisfactory proof that she has had the benefit of that piece of paper. Hansom, hi!"

They were out on the door-step, the door was closed behind them, and the doctor bounded into a cab.

"Curse the snow!"

Whew! how the white sheet turned and twisted, and drifted wildly to and fro, in its efforts to lie spread evenly over everything alike, if the wind would but let it. That was exactly what the wind would not do, however, blowing it down from roofs and steeples into the streets and squares below : then, having got it there, it tossed the flaky mass about in mad helter-skelter fashion, giving it no rest till every nook was piled with quivering and sullied shreds. But the patient snow kept falling, and quietly draped the boisterous havoc with its increasing folds. At last the wind could do no more to keep the ground clear, and betook itself with many an empty parting growl of menace to the higher regions, where there was rare sport for it still (ho, ho !) in defending the summits of churches, public buildings, and all lofty erections from the intruder's feathery encroachments. Gradually even these were seized and covered, however ; and when the very telegraph-wires hung heavy with the insidious enemy's long white lines, the poor wind itself, uttering a last feeble wail of protest, was speedily buried alive.

" Curse the snow !" repeated Lorton to himself, treading it savagely under his cruel heel as he trudged along. He had no umbrella, and only wore his ordinary coarse tweed jacket. It was not surprising, therefore, that he should shiver every now and then : exercise should have warmed him, but it did not ; his shivering fits continued.

" A touch of ague," he muttered querulously :

"haven't had such a thing since the first winter after I came back. Gad, I must try to stave it off this time ; must get some quinine to-morrow."

He went into the next public-house he passed, and called for a plentiful allowance of raw spirit. The beverage had a soothing, not to say exhilarating effect, and he bethought him that he had not dined or supped that evening. He ordered a plate of cold meat, and some bread and cheese, changing Paston's note to pay for it. The bar was warm and cheerful, the landlord argumentative, and the liquor good. Lorton took his time over the meal, sitting a good while longer after it was over to imbibe the mingled grog and eloquence of the house. Thus it was midnight before he turned, in a state of temporary cheerfulness, into the street where his lodgings were situated.

It was very dark, and even if it had not been, the snow would have made it difficult to see anything a short distance off.

He did not, however, feel the inconvenience of this quite so much as another wanderer who happened at this identical moment to be tending in the same direction.

Anathematising the weather freely under his breath, which was rather short, this person quickened his pace, and following Lorton up his doorstep squeezed past him into the passage.

" Hullo ! What the—"

"Didn't you expect me ? " interrupted the other panting ; " but of course you didn't ; how could you ? "

He removed a soft, high-crowned felt hat to shake off the snow which gave it something of the appearance of a miniature alp, revealing by this act the curiously-carved figure-head apper-taining to Hiram Rock, bookseller.

His old friend and associate led the way into the little parlour and closed the door.

" Why have you tracked me here ? " he demanded, stifling an oath.

Mr. Rock made an ineffectual attempt to warm his hands at the dead embers in the grate before replying :

" You see, my boy, things haven't been going quite smoothly with me since you left me to bear the brunt of it all alone ; so I concluded to try a change. Copesbury is a dull place for a man like me to bury himself in all the year round. We old travellers are afraid of getting a bit musty unless we can get an occasional rub in society, eh ? " He gave a strident chuckle, adding : " I enquired at the old place, and found you were enjoying yourself like a lord ; so I thought I'd come and help you to put in a convivial time."

" I'm sorry you should have had your trouble

for nothing, Mr. Rock; but I must ask you
to sneak out again by the way you sneaked in.
They probably don't keep a night-porter at your
hotel, and may be getting nervous at your
prolonged absence. Now then, are you going?"
The voice in which Lorton asked this question
was choked with passion.

"No," was his venerable guest's reply, as he
sat down very composedly; "since you ask me,
I don't intend to expose myself needlessly to
the night air, thank you. As to my reason for
dropping in upon you—shouldn't think you
could have more convenient quarters, by the
way— I don't want to intrude business just
now, it being rather late, as you say; but you
mustn't run away with the idea that our little
deed of partnership is cancelled yet. It may
be a dark deed," cried the bookseller in accents
of regret, "but that is all the more reason why
it should be kept so."

He stopped to observe the effect of this
subtlety upon his companion.

"However, 'pleasure first' is my motto,"
he concluded, divesting himself of his streaming
coat.

Lorton tried to steady his feverish brain.
Clearly it would not do to offend his former
colleague, who might, for aught he knew,
possess the means of crushing him without

further ado.   It seemed hard that he could
not fleece others without getting fleeced for it
himself; but there was no help for it; at
present he was too muddled to see anything
clearly.

"Make yourself at home," he said at last with
a dismal pretence of cordiality.  "I—I—you took
me by surprise, and I've been badgered enough
for one day ; we can talk to-morrow."

"Of course we can," was the equally frank
response ;  "I made sure you wouldn't have
the heart to turn me out in the cold."

He took a flat bottle from his pocket, and
drained the contents.

"Now," said Hiram, smacking his lips, "if
you can give me a bed I should prefer it to
the floor."

Lorton vacantly conducted him up-stairs into
the room which had received its humble preparations for Ursula.               .

"What! keeps an extra bedroom for his
friend!  Thoughtfulness like this is touching to
an old man who has roamed about the selfish
world for more than threescore years, and
seldom met with such a mark of forethought.
Between those sheets I shall soon forget all
my cares, rocked in Murphy's arms, as the
poet says."

But in spite of this complimentary ebullition,

there was an enquiring, not .to say suspicious, look on his face as he parted from his kind host for the night.

Lorton could not sleep: the soporific effects of the spirits ceased as soon as his head touched the pillow, and returning ague prevented him from throwing off the unwonted anxieties which were agitating his mind. He could not forget Paston's warning voice, do what he would. He tried stopping his ears, but their imperviousness to every other sound only seemed to make the doctor's words come back more distinctly than ever. "Your daughter will starve before she will be made the excuse for asking any one to support you. You were a fool not to see that before you undertook to provide for two mouths instead of one." Louder and louder the words sounded, taking a higher, more importunate pitch at each repetition; till at last they rose into a jingling screech, causing him to start convulsively into a sitting posture with a smothered cry of despair.

It was true, every bit of it. Clod-witted idiot that he had been! He had reckoned upon Ursula bringing grist to his impoverished mill in any case, but she could not do so all at once. Engagements on the stage—where there was a chance of promotion—were as difficult to get as engagements elsewhere: and he could not wait. Still less could he afford to do so now that Rock had turned up to sponge upon him. In the few hours since he had seen Paston the necessity of shutting another mouth—a most insatiable one—had been laid upon him. In his bodily suffering his mind refused to review the matter calmly : he altogether missed over one alternative, — which was indeed the true one — namely, that the bookseller was solely speculating upon a contingency at present un-realised.

That misunderstood tradesman had made up his mind to decline the humiliating terms offered to him by Robur through Mr. Armitage. The proposed surveillance was not only galling to his independent spirit,—it was a check to his turning any little profits outside his ostensible business. Now Hiram foresaw much difficulty in making the needful two ends meet under these painful circumstances : the vending of mis-cellaneous literature without any prospect of such small pickings as might accrue to him under cover of that respectable vocation held out promises far from lucrative. He had therefore quitted the Bœotian atmosphere of Copesbury, omitting to mention his purpose to his few friends and customers there, and found himself in London, safe from persecution, but empty in pocket and somewhat undecided upon his next move. Intuition, however, came to his assistance, with the result of bringing about a welcome encounter with the quondam sharer of his cares and—gains. The juncture turned out to be a peculiarly lucky one: if Lorton had nothing to give him at present, he was at least expecting a financial *coup*, or what was the meaning of these extensive preparations? His host, too, was evidently afraid of him, and prepared to buy his silence—not about the past (they were both in the same plight as to that), but with respect to some plan to be accomplished in the immediate future. Rock's cool demeanour and reticence had secured him against the repulse which otherwise he must have sustained, an entrance being thereby effected which he fully intended should last.

"Say nothing, and pick up all I can is the ticket," he muttered to himself, as he descended to breakfast.

Lorton did not return his cheery greeting; there was an expression on his jaded face which the observant elder did not remember to have noticed there the previous night.

"What's he at now?" he wondered; "if he's plotting to get rid of me I must counterplot, I suppose."

Acting upon this sound maxim he took occasion to grumble out something about an engagement

at the other end of the town, which would keep
him from opening the business just then.

" But I hope to be back again this evening,"
added he, " and we can have it out comfortab'y
before bedtime. Deuce take that Robur chap ;
what does he want to lug me out for, a morning
like this, I should like to know ? "

The other paying no apparent attention to his
wilfully misleading remark, Mr. Rock arrayed
himself in walking panoply, and departed ;
making what he could of a meeting with the
garrulous landlady on his way out of the house.

Lorton remained long as the bookseller had
left him, plunged in a deep and gloomy reverie.
He was not sorry to postpone the business,
whatever it was, which his guest had to tell
him of. For reasons of his own Mr. Rock's
temporary absence was grateful to him ; it was
a godsend. The intruder's excuse for going
signified little ;—what was it ? something about
—he had forgotten, had never heard it at all, so
entirely did the thought that his companion *was*
going possess him. As a matter of fact, he did
not expect that he should ever gaze upon that
disagreeably familiar form again. Difficulties
were accumulating, and he was free to fly : a
hundred sighing voices whispered round him,
urging him to take the step. He would obey,
he would take it.

He was not a fanciful man :—perhaps it was
the ague,—but a superstitious terror had something to do with his last resolve. What if he
were going to fall seriously ill ! He thought of
the workhouse infirmary, and shuddered : it was
too much for a man of his refined susceptibilities.
But his thoughts did not stop there; they
hurried him on to depths beyond even those to
which parochial assistance extends. He heard
the tap-tap of the hammer, the swish of the
plane, and, sick and giddy, felt himself already
within the roughly constructed shell. Vainly
he strove to break through the delusion. All
was black now, and the rattle of loose mould
and stones drowned his muffled screams.
Enough ! He could feel the sweat starting out
all over him. He rose panting; it was settled;
under a warmer sky he would recover health
and spirits.

Then he considered how he was to get away.
He would meet Ursula; that was a treat not
to be foregone. Besides, he must get that ring
again, and anything else in the way of money
or valuables she might happen to have with
her; they would be useful to him abroad, and
he had only between four and five pounds in his
pocket. Then he would bring or send her to
their lodgings, making his escape unperceived
before Rock returned.

He could laugh now, and did so at the idea of leaving them both in the lurch to mourn his disappearance. She would have to beg for money to pay off the week's rent anyhow.

Time to start for the station. He was to meet her at three o'clock by the refreshment-bar. With cruel deliberation he had appointed that as their trysting-place; and now his paternal forethought cautioned him against hurrying, for fear the train might have been delayed, and so he might be disappointed of seeing the girl in this novel situation.

" Curse the snow ! "

Still it descended, an emblem of the angelic pity that would seek, in spite of all rebuffs, to shroud men's evil works beneath some garb of innocence.

But to Lorton it conveyed no such tender reproof. Keeping his head bent with sullen obstinacy, and looking to neither side, he made his way along the slippery streets, dogged by fleeting shadows. One shape more substantial than the rest kept him persistently in sight. Mr. Rock's engagements were not too pressing to allow of his keeping watch and ward over his shifty friend. For some way the unconscious object of pursuit kept well ahead: it was not until he crossed the teeming thoroughfare opposite the station, and struck into its precincts that the spy, uttering an exclamation of chagrin, mended his pace.

"He's going to give me the slip, after all, and bolt," murmured Mr. Rock plaintively. "If I can only find out where he takes his ticket for, a telegram would stop him when he gets there, and I don't care what they do to me, as long as I can take it out of him."

The thought of his friend being arrested directly he stepped out of the train was so eminently fascinating that he was about to still further increase his speed, when it was completely arrested by a strange ominous whizzing, and a sudden cry so appalling that the little crowd of foot-passengers involuntarily drew together, and horses started in a short stampede.

There must have been a great catastrophe, surely, to occasion this commotion.

But the scene had not changed except in one slight particular.

Something hung in a loose curling mesh from a pent-house not very far above, a thread in the rigid web which seemed to net in almost the whole of that open space : the tension had been too great for the thread, and it was severed. What difference did this make to anybody ?

None, probably, by this time ; for there in the middle of the road, where Lorton had been crossing the moment before, lay stiffening a grim unsightly mass on which the flakes fell sadly.

Who shall say that the life's electric current was not sundered from its fleshly medium by a Divine Hand, or that the wire had not that day been freighted with the late message of a just Omnipotence, more merciful as well as more severe than man's puny retaliation?

But, be the truth what it may, that iniquity should be punished by iniquity is, happily, not one of the laws of the universe.

As for the sordid clay within a yard or two of Ursula's feet, between its departed soul and her whom her dead father had known so imperfectly, time infinitely small had set a gulf which only eternity may bridge.

# CHAPTER XII.

### INSIDE THE STATION.

"There are tears for the many,
And pleasures for the few;
But let the world pass on, dear,
There's love for me and you."—*Hood.*

WE left Aunt Joan and Arnold in consternation at Ursula's unforeseen flight: the last project for her safety, if not for her deliverance, had been defeated by the girl herself. What was to be done?

The sight of Joanna's suffering made her companion restrain any expression of his own grief and dismay from escaping his lips.

"I will follow her," he said resolutely; adding in a voice so low that it was scarcely audible, "Who knows? I may find her yet."

Joanna was speechless: she only nodded, motioning to him to lose no time: and without another word he left her.

On arriving breathless at the station he found that the slow train for London had started some few minutes before. He looked for Ursula's luggage; it had gone.

The next train—the one she was to have travelled by originally— was the mid-day express, which was timed to reach its destination at three o'clock, not quite half-an-hour after Ursula would be set down there. Good: possibly Lorton would not be punctual at the rendezvous; or, at any rate, they could be overtaken and kept in sight.

He went back to the hotel for his bag, deciding not to show himself again to Joanna. He could not help her, and perhaps her suspense would be easier if she fancied he was already on his way.

The train was still moving along the platform at the end of its journey when he sprang out, and looked wildly round for his mistress.

Not a trace of her was to be seen. He enquired eagerly for her, thereby occasioning much chaffing comment among the blue-faced porters. One of them volunteering the information in a surly tone that he had seen a young lady in the refreshment-room a short time back, and farther giving it as his unqualified opinion that it was " the best place, too, for them as had any coppers to spend," Arnold hurried off distractedly to look there.

He was faint and weary with excitement, and besides had hardly tasted food that day.

The barmaid eyed him across the counter with bold curiosity not unmingled with suspicion.

" Take your orders, sir ? "

He took up some eatable, the first that came to hand.

" Eh ? yes," he replied, half-unconscious of what he was about.

She shrugged her shoulders, and put a glass of sherry and bitters before him, honouring him the while with another broad stare.

Then she resumed the thread of a conversation which she had apparently been carrying on with a party somewhat advanced in years, who was endeavouring to resuscitate his dilapidated fascinations by the internal application of a glass of steaming negus.

Meanwhile Arnold looked round the place. There was nothing to guide him in his search, however. In one corner a bloated woman in draggled black silk and ostrich feathers was brushing biscuit-crumbs from her dress with one hand, while with the other she clinked a spoon against the tumbler which she had just set down empty. A child in a gaudy frock a size or so too large for her sat opposite this voluminous matron, scraping together with grimy fingers certain evidences of a stale sponge-cake that strewed the marble top of the table before her. Then there were one or two seedy young men in brown coats and hats,—the latter with brims more or less broad and flat,—smoking cigars cheap enough, but no cheaper than they should have been, and discussing in a nasal accent some subject consisting in great measure of a jargon of unintelligible allusions. Fly-blown notices and advertisements decorated the walls, relieved at intervals by flaring and flickering gas-lamps which made the long rows of bottles at the back of the bar shine with a dull, fitful glimmer. It would be hard to say which was most oppressive— the pestiferous air of this particularly unrefreshing room, or its squalid cheerlessness.

To think that he could have expected to find Ursula in this dreadful place !

He finished what he was eating, and tried to catch the barmaid's attention in order to pay her. But she happened to be engrossed in reciting some interesting narrative to her faded admirer.

Arnold was obliged to listen, and overheard the following fragment :

"Well, in she comes, as I was sayin', a bit nervous, you know, just for all the world as if I wasn't good enough for her (don't do that, sir): I see she was lookin' for someone ; so I says to her, ' Will you have anything now, Miss, or wait till he comes ? ' She looks at me surprised : ' Has he been here, then ? ' she asks. Lor, you

never see sich bloomin' innercence. ' Who d'yer
mean ?' says I. 'My father,' says she. ' He
ain't been here yet,' says I, ' and if I was you I'd
jest step into the waitin' room till 'e does come,
'cos I'll tell him you're there, and 'e can come
and fetch you himself.' "

" Is she in there now, my dear ?" enquired the
owner of the fascinations aforesaid.

" Come now, what do you ask that for ?" was
his wanton charmer's rejoinder. " No, she ain't ;
I s'pose it didn't suit her better than in 'ere : I
see her go outside somewhere jest now. 'I've no
patience with them dressmakin' gals as always
dresses that mean and quiet they won't even
wear a bit of coloured ribbon in their 'air, nor
no jew'lry, not even a locket round their neck.
Pretty? oh yes, I s'pose so. Now don't go
a-pinchin' of me, 'cos I can't abide you, and I
won't allow it."

Arnold paid, and took his departure.

He thought he would go to the cloak-room to
make enquiries there and leave his bag. In
order to accomplish his intention it was necessary
to go outside the station and round a corner of
it. He was in the act of emerging from the
dark entrance into the open space in front, when
there was a sudden dispersion of men and horses
in it, the people on the pavement forming
instinctively into a cowering knot.

"A man struck down !" "Where ?" "By what ?"

The meaningless buzz fell unheeded on his ears, for close in front of him stood motionless the form of her whom he loved,—motionless but for an instant. She turned her face—he had only time to drop all else from his hands, and receive her swooning in his arms.

A moment's brief sweetness and she had rallied, turning on him " the star-like sorrows of immortal eyes" in troubled wonderment.

No one noticed the pair ; they were all intent upon that other thing.

Arnold gave her his arm, and she clung to it trembling.

" There ; " she pointed to the people clustering in the road,—for they had left the pavement now —" I was waiting for him—he saw me—he was coming, and—" She could not go on : her whole frame shuddered, but she was silent.

He took her into the hotel, telling her that Aunt Joan had sent him, and that she would wish it. A chambermaid was told off to conduct Ursula to a private sitting-room, with instructions to light a fire and attend to her wants generally.

Then Arnold went to find out what had actually happened to Lorton.

The weight of the snow had increased the

normal strain upon the telegraph and other wires that were stretched across the approach to the railway. One of them had snapped, and striking against Lorton with frightful force, inflicted wounds which were almost immediately fatal. A stretcher was brought, and the police carried off the body. Arnold first despatched a telegram to Joanna, bidding her come up to join Ursula at all costs that evening; then he went to find out what arrangements were being made about the inquest. Through his instrumentality the remains were identified later by Dr. Paston and Mr. Bloss, the Editor of the *Tuba*, as those of Edward Edwards, Esq., formerly advertising manager and assistant editor of that prominent journal.

Arnold was back again in time to meet Aunt Joan at the station shortly before eight. She was soon in possession of all he had to tell her, being considerably more affected at his simple account of how he met Ursula than at the intelligence of her father's unlooked-for demise. Before she went to the girl Arnold told her that he would settle everything connected with the funeral, if she would consent to take her charge back to Burnport on the morrow; and this she promised to do, pressing his hand gratefully.

When they parted he returned to Paston, resolving not to inconvenience them by his presence at the hotel, though the thought of voluntarily declining to remain under the same roof with Ursula was sufficiently irksome. Still, that was nothing compared with the deep joy of knowing that now at last, in his case, too, love had broken down all barriers (Armitage's words) between two faithful hearts.

When the doctor came in from a professional visit he found his friend looking better, in spite of his long day, than he had seen him since the time when they used to lounge on "the Backs" or take a pull up the " Freshers' " river together.

" Ah, you're happy now, aren't you ? " observed Paston, clearing his throat severely to conceal something uncommonly like a sigh—only that this serene personage was never heard to sigh. " I begin to think there's nothing like your pre-scription for curing the ills, physical and mental, of mortals. I only wish you could impart the formula to me. Bless you, I'd make my fortune in no time out of love-philtres."

" Do you remember that night at Oakleigh when I asked you to find me a lever for opening the world-oyster ? " said Arnold.

" Yes, and I thought I had given you one. Haven't I seen you using it on one or two occa-sions since then ? Why, you've even recom-mended levers of the same pattern to others of your friends in my hearing. Don't tell me I had nothing to do with your getting your chaos of ideas into some sort of order, Robur; I helped you when you couldn't see the wood for the trees; and are you going to cut me because you can see your way out without my farther assistance?"

"Certainly not, my dear man; your lever is an excellent one, and will do you more credit in my hands than it has yet done, if I may make a prophecy. At the same time, you must admit that a lever isn't much good without a fulcrum, and as you omitted to supply me with that I had to look about for one on my own account. Hitherto this fulcrum of mine has been far from stable, and so your tool hadn't a fair chance of proving its capability: the future must decide whether it or the workman is at fault."

"How are you going to make the experiment? Why, my dear fellow, I suppose (to drop allegory) you'll be marrying and 'settling down,' as they say, next. 'The funeral baked meats,' etcetera;" there was a malicious twinkle in the doctor's eye as he left Arnold to mentally complete the quotation.

"I see what you mean," returned Robur, smiling at the innocent wickedness of this last remark: "once married, a man is bound to find the solution of his difficulties in conjugal union, or pretend to do so, even if he doesn't. Well, well; I intend to give *my* love a fairer trial than

that. A year hence, should the progress which
is begun here develope my faculties and insight
as it ought, then I shall seek to marry,—not,
indeed, for the purpose of settling down, but
rather for incitement to farther objects of ambition than I could reach, or even dream of
reaching, alone."

"Ah ; " the doctor allowed the regulation
interval to pass before proceeding : "an unusual
step, but methinks a wise one. Long engagements are generally a mere matter of pecuniary
necessity, and the shortest of them are regulated
more by the time it takes to provide a trousseau
than that requisite for the lovers to get at a clear
mutual understanding. Some people might say
it was hard on the girl, though."

"Not if they knew her," said Robur, smiling.

# CHAPTER XIII,

## WHOLESALE BUSINESS

" Pray you, no more of this : 'tis like the howling of Irish
wolves against the moon."—*As You Like It.*

THE next day Joanna and Ursula returned to
Burnport. It was agreed that there was no
reason why Ursula should remain for the funeral.
To her father, while he was still living, she had
felt that she owed a debt of duty which even his
heartlessness had not sufficed to cancel; and
the fact of her mother having given him up for
her child's sake made the girl feel that duty all
the more binding. So she had acted according
to a high if somewhat quixotic sense of right in
leaving her dearest friend with the hope of doing
something to purify and elevate her father's life.
But now that the father himself was no more,
now that the slender hope his daughter had
cherished was placed beyond the reach of realisation, a pretence of affection would have been

mere mockery, and the funeral itself would have
been a trial which Ursula, after the series of
shocks she had lately undergone, was ill-fitted to
endure. So Miss Blunsden with her charge left
town by an early train.

Miss Hilda had been greatly disturbed by the
many commotions of the previous day. The
good lady had found her nerves so sadly dis-
composed in the morning that she had retired
into the privacy of her chamber to consume
those light medicines which she always found so
helpful on these occasions, and to meditate on
the vanity of human affairs, the perversity of
the weather, and the obstinacy of her sister and
niece. Had it been possible, Joanna would have
refrained from disturbing her on receiving
Arnold's telegram; but so unusual a proceeding
as the younger sister's sudden departure for the
metropolis, with all the consequences that would
be involved, could not be passed over in silence.
There is no record as to what Miss Blunsden did
or thought when she received the startling
intelligence of Lorton's death ; but she had
managed to recover considerably when Joanna
and Ursula returned.

They found her seated in the parlour engaged
in giving a finishing touch to the locks that
surrounded St. Guthlac's tonsure ; herself arrayed
in a chaste robe of mourning. Her eyes lighted

on Ursula's face : for a moment sympathy over-
came her dreary and insipid selfishness ; she rose
and kissed the girl with affection, even with
warmth. Joanna, to her own intense surprise,
fancied she saw something very like a tear glisten
in her sister's eye. But it was for a moment
only ; hardly had the Mother Superior given
place to the woman, before the passing warmth
froze again, and the woman was once more
nothing but a Mother Superior. Such ebullitions
of feeling, Miss Hilda was aware, are unbecoming. She must atone for her weakness.

"My dear child, this is a sad blow to us all ;
you especially must strive to endure it with
resignation. And it is the sadder," continued
she—having apparently recalled to mind that
there were doubtful passages in the life of the
late Mr. Lorton—"it is the sadder because your
father was cut off thus suddenly, for aught
we can see, in the midst of——"

"Hilda, hold your tongue."

It is an astonishing fact, but Miss Hilda
obeyed ; for the time principally because she
was too startled by her sister's assumption of
authority to do anything else. Aunt Joan retired in triumph with Ursula ; but she was not
absent long. She returned to find Miss Blunsden rehabilitating herself with smelling salts.
Whereupon she sat down and gave that good

lady such a "talking to" as she had never
experienced in her life before, the upshot of
which was that Miss Hilda was never again
heard to name Mr. Lorton, and submitted completely in all matters relating to Ursula. For
the first time in all her days she had made
Joanna thoroughly angry, and she did not dare
to do it again. In other respects the little
household returned to their former way of life.

As for Arnold, his time during the next few
months was variously occupied. East London
was a field where his energies found plenty of
material to expend themselves on. It cannot be
said that he produced any very astonishing
results; but he felt that such work as he could
get to do called for the careful exercise of his
higher faculties, and his sympathies were keenly
awakened. Something he certainly did towards
brightening the lives of a few families, and here
and there inspiring his friends among the arti-
sans with higher ideals and clearer principles
than they had known before, and a sounder
knowledge of the facts of life; and his own
ideas of the life among these classes, vague and
ill-defined before, received a much clearer shape,
and he felt that his labour was by no means
thrown away. He had gained an insight into
the real wants and needs of these men such
as not very many persons in his own rank of

life possess ; and he had sown seeds which might some day bring forth fruit. Here then he spent the greater part of the twelve months of probation which he had allotted for himself, though he was not neglectful of his duties at Oakleigh, such as they were.

As for Mr. Hiram Rock, bookseller, that worthy vanished completely. Apparently he was not penniless, for one morning his miscellaneous library was removed from Copesbury under the superintendence of a young man wearing a battered billy-cock very much on one side of his head, who found time to ogle an occasional nursemaid. It was understood that this young gentleman was the representative of Messrs. Worm and Parchment, a noted firm of second-hand book-vendors in a very grimy quarter of the metropolis. On being questioned he averred, with very precarious use of the letter h, that he "didn't knäow hanythink abäout the party as sold the books, but wot 'e did knäow was, that the guv'nors were wäit'n for 'em, an' 'e 'ad'n' got no täime to wäist a-jawrin'."

Mr. Rock, it appeared, had taken prompt measures after his interview with the Canon to ensure the sale of his mouldy volumes, and had vanished with the proceeds. The presumption is that he crossed the Atlantic at an early date, trusting to his fluency and address to secure a means of livelihood in America. It is not unlikely that one of the States has by this time provided him, under an alias, with board and lodging in return for his services in the oakum department: as it can hardly be expected that he developed any fresh inclinations to honesty at his advanced years. At any rate, no search was made for him in England, as Lorton's connexion with him made it impossible for Arnold to prosecute. The books were removed to commodious quarters in London; a new occupant was found for the shop where Mr. Rock had dwelt, and the old gentleman's place knew him no more.

The twelve months were almost at an end, when Paston came down to Oakleigh again to visit Arnold and talk over many things.

The two friends sat in the library together after breakfast, and chatted at first vaguely, discussing the affairs of the nation, and various projects in the East End of London now getting gradually formulated. But both of them felt that this was not the subject they really had at heart just then, greatly though they were both interested in it. The talk died down presently, and the two men sat in silence for some time. Then Paston spoke.

" Well, Robur, your year is pretty nearly out

now. You have been waiting, and working pretty hard; and, upon my word, I think you're vastly the better for it."

"My dear fellow, don't go fishing for compliments. I'm quite prepared to admit that you were primarily responsible for any improvement in me, inasmuch as you sent me to Burnport. But your medicine wouldn't have done by itself."

"Well, upon my soul! Here's gratitude. What was it I told you to do? Find employment and face your difficulties. How did I tell you to do it? Go to Burnport. Well, you have done what I told you, in the way I told you—and now you want to appropriate the honour of my brilliant cure."

Arnold laughed. "Far be it from me to claim the honours: but they're due to a better doctor than you, after all, old man."

"H'm. Such is the reward the blameless leach receives at the hands of shameless sons of mortals. But I grant you that I didn't calculate on the lady. Certainly she deserves an M.D. for her successful treatment."

Arnold rose and walked to the window, from which he addressed his companion without turning round.

"Chaffing is all very well, Paston. I can't thank you enough for the encouragement you gave me when I came back to England fifteen months ago, and your excellent remark about classifying the devil. But there is some one, but for whom that advice of yours, good as it was, would have had very little effect. You don't know what this has been to me. Then I was like a man in a fog, who took every light for a will-o'-the-wisp. Now——"

"I remember," said the doctor meditatively, "I remember the time when I should have been rather inclined to pity you for such a remark. I didn't much believe in women—they are so exceedingly annoying when you want to find out their symptoms. But I have rather changed my views on that point. *Inductio per enumerationem simplicem* overthrown by one contrary instance. Now I could mention as contrary instances Miss Joanna Blunsden, and on your authority, Miss Lorton, and one or two others perhaps. I don't include the whole sex in my condemnation."

"Your condescension is delightful; however, you would have a poorish time of it if you didn't allow an occasional exception to your general rule. By the way, I am going over to Beau Séjour in the course of the afternoon. Do you feel inclined to pay your respects over there?"

"I don't mind if I do," said Paston with a careless air; "how are the family? What's become of my young friend Frank?"

"Frank?" said Arnold, coming back and taking up his stand by the fire: "oh, he seems to be getting on well enough. He went off to Texas, with an apparent desire to turn over a new leaf; and, in fact, he came to me of his own accord before he had even made up his mind to go, to apologise and that sort of thing. I thought it an excellent sign; there must be some good at the bottom of him or he wouldn't have done it; and from what I hear, he seems to be keeping steady and working pretty hard. Grace is very cheerful about him; he used to be a burden on her mind, poor girl."

"Ah. Miss Dalton hasn't found anyone to marry her yet?"

"No," said Arnold.

They went over together that afternoon to Beau Séjour. They found the whole family together, and were promptly greeted with the announcement that a letter had that morning arrived from Texas.

"Poor dear boy, Arnold, I'm sure it's very good of him to settle down and work so hard, and I do think the way young men seem to have to work is dreadful, and Frank never could manage it in England. I'm sure I only wonder they don't all get brain fever, what with all the books and things. Not but what it's quite as bad out there, and I know I'm always expecting

to hear that Frank or Willie have got sun-
stroke or something. Don't you think so, Mr.
Paston ?"

The doctor had not the dimmest notion what
it was that Mrs. Dalton wanted him to acquiesce
in. So he paused, and gave vent to a professional "Quite so." Happily the lady was
satisfied. However, at this point her husband
broke in.

"Look here, Arnold, did ever you see a letter
like that?" and he held up the document for
public inspection. "Bless my soul! There's a
fist for a man to write! 'Deed, it's a good thing
your brother didn't have a try at Sandhurst,
Grace, for he'd have been ploughed as sure as
eggs is eggs. Just look at it. There's spelling
for you! That's what he learns by going out
there, is it?"

"Well, papa, he didn't go there to learn spelling," said Grace.

"And who said he did? Excuse me, Mr.
Paston, or Dr. Paston, I believe I should say,
but being a man of science you are doubtless
aware that these young people give themselves
the most unconscionable airs."

"I don't know whether you're including me
in that sweeping denunciation, Mr. Dalton: I
haven't got grey-headed yet, you know."

"Papa wants an ally, that's all," said Grace;

" and he thinks he'll win you over by complimenting you on your sage appearance."

" Well then," suggested Arnold, " you'd better
put in a bid to secure Paston on your own side.
You've no notion what an admirer of the sex he
is, Grace; to look at him, you might put him
down for a misogynist. But he's given up his
evil ways, and you can turn him round your little
finger now, I believe—if you'll only bid high
enough at first."

Grace was puzzled; so, as the safest way out
of the difficulty, she laughed.

But Mrs. Dalton had been silent too long.
She had been taking in the fact that Paston was
entitled to the complimentary title.

" Dear me ; and so you're really a doctor now,
Mr. Paston, that is, Doctor Paston: but I didn't
know doctors were ever so young, you know.
And now I want to know if you really think it's
right for Arnold to be going about in that dreadful East End the way he does. Of course it's
very good of him, and all that sort of thing,
giving up his time to these people, though what
he wants to do it for I'm sure I don't know.
People never did that sort of thing in my young
days, and it seems to me very foolish, what with
small-pox and scarlatina, and goodness knows if
we shan't be having cholera over here some of
these days."

Paston listened with apparent attention to this harangue ; but his eyes, it seemed, were engaged in another quarter. Grace rose to put some coals on the fire ; she had been trained by practical necessity to do all these little offices, and Frank's society had taught her that the other sex were not to be relied on as substitutes. But Paston forestalled her, and there was a little bit of an argument before she could give in, and altogether it was some time before the doctor was able to answer Mrs. Dalton's observations. Indeed, it is rather creditable to him that when he returned to his seat he had some notion of what the good lady had been talking about. He was proceeding to assure her that Robur's health was by no means seriously endangered by his philanthropy, when the door opened and Canon Armitage was announced. The result was that there was a general uprising and hand-shaking, and a kind of "General Post," to borrow a metaphor from one of the most popular of juvenile games ; and somehow Paston found himself seated by Grace, with Armitage between him and the lady of the house.

The Canon's appearance had not undergone much alteration. Perhaps he looked a trifle more ecclesiastical, if that be possible, than when last we saw him. He had been a great success at Copesbury, and had won golden opinions from every quarter since his appointment, and was looked upon generally as a coming man. He had published a pamphlet on the question of Disestablishment, which was considered a masterpiece of skilful argument combined with unwonted tact and moderation ; and he had preached before very eminent personages. Otherwise there was little to say about him, save that he seemed no nearer marrying than he had been fifteen months before.

Mrs. Dalton descended upon him with startling celerity.

"Such a long time since we've seen you, Canon Armitage ; I declare I wonder you haven't been made a bishop since, only of course we've seen you at Burfield." She forgot completely that the Canon had been present at the Christmas festivities only seven weeks back, and had dined at Beau Séjour since, so that the interval for his promotion was small. "But there, I'm sure you're looking as if you'd been overworking yourself dreadfully. You ought to marry, and have a wife to take care of you."

Mr. Dalton heard, and chuckled. "Too much sense, haven't you, Armitage ? It's just for all the world like buying a pig in a poke is marrying, take my word for it." His remark, however, was lost on his better half, who never attempted to follow his proverbial philosophy.

"But I declare, you men never know how to take care of yourselves properly. There's Arnold

Robur working himself to death down in the East End, with all sorts of cholera and things going on all round, and Doctor Paston actually encouraging him. I think it's really dreadful, you know, Canon Armitage, and I do wish you'd speak to him about it. He might listen to you, but I'm sure it's no use *my* talking to him."

"Certainly," said the wily Canon, "I expect to have a good deal to say to Robur about his experiences in London," which was a diplomatic and deceitful way of putting it, because it left Mrs. Dalton under the impression that he was going to do as she asked him.

Paston had by this time got fixed in a conversation about flowers with Grace; Arnold and Mr. Dalton were having a quiet discussion in a corner, the subject of which is of no importance to anybody; and so Armitage and Mrs. Dalton settled down into a *tête-à-tête*, and it was really a study to observe the amount of attention the gentleman seemed to bestow on the talking partner in the firm—if that expression is permissible. She, good soul, unaccustomed to such treatment, poured forth her streams of eloquence with redoubled volubility; and the clergyman really felt it an intense relief to be able to chuckle inwardly when he heard on his left,

"Haven't you ever seen one ?"

" No, Miss Dalton, I'm afraid not. Have you got any here ? "

" Oh yes ; there are several in the conservatory."

And he was not surprised to observe, shortly after the tea came in, that Miss Grace was going to show the Doctor the unknown flower. ꞏ

" Robur," he said presently, " I'm going over your way to see one or two sick folks ; will you give me your company ? "

" Humph ! And what are you going to do with Paston, may I ask ? " enquired the unconscious Mr. Dalton.

It was wonderful to see the air of practised deception with which the reverend Canon replied that a stern necessity required his own immediate departure ; but that he wanted to talk privately with Robur, and Paston might overtake them, as he knew his way. Arnold agreed in his view of the case ; and they bade farewell to Mr. and Mrs. Dalton.

" I say, Armitage," said Robur, as soon as they got outside, " what does all this mean ? why, he hasn't seen her half-a-dozen times."

Armitage broke out into an exceedingly hearty fit of laughter.

" Well, he has kept pretty quiet ; but are you quite sure of your half-dozen ? "

" Why, what d' you mean ? "

"My dear fellow, I mean simply this—that circumstances brought me across Paston after that first meeting of ours here, and we rather took to each other. You didn't notice the warmth of his greeting to me to-day? It would have been rather odd if we hadn't met since. We took to each other, as I say; and Paston has on sundry occasions received me very hospitably at Wimpole Street, and the hospitality has been now and then reciprocated."

"You mean that he has stopped with you when I've been over in Whitechapel?"

"Precisely," said the other, chuckling afresh.

"Why, he never said a word of it to me," said Arnold, stopping and looking at his companion.

"No doubt—nor did I till now, because he particularly begged me not to. But that is how I found out what was going on, and why I put that exceedingly severe strain on my conscience this afternoon. The murder's out now. Don't tell him I let you know."

"Upon my word!" said Arnold; "and this man is a dignitary of the Church!"

They walked on in silence for a few minutes, and Arnold turned on his companion again with a smile.

"I say, Armitage, I never expected you to take a paternal interest in such exceedingly

mundane matters as love-affairs. We shall be
hearing that you're engaged yourself presently."

The clerical Ananias laughed; but his voice
was grave again when he answered, " I don't
think that's likely, Robur. Marriage isn't included in my theory of my own life; but I
should be the last to look upon it as a mundane
subject. Doubtless it has a side which belongs
to comedy, but its other side is worthy of treatment in an Epic. Love, as I take it, is one of
the highest emotions of which man is capable;
and the love of a man and woman ought to be
the emotion's highest form—for some minds, at
any rate. Some seem incapable of it; some seem
to find their best sphere in other thoughts, in
labouring for humanity."

" Do the two ideas clash then? Surely not.
A man's love doesn't take the heart out of his
work, unless I'm very much mistaken."

" No," said the clergyman, " I would not say
that; but that there are some persons who seem
to be without need of any single human love:
whose hearts, as it were, embrace all mankind.
Yet, down at bottom I half suspect that they are
no gainers by that—while I confess that I myself
never feel the craving for another self, a heart
which must beat in answer to my own."

" Truly," replied Arnold, " I think they are
indeed losers—these solitary souls. And yet we

number among them some of the men whom posterity loves above all others. But for myself, Armitage, do you know about me?"

"I have heard nothing since you stayed with me," said the other; "are you—" He paused.

"To-morrow," said Robur, "I am going down to Burnport; and when I return, I trust it will be merely to make such preparations as are needful before—well, Armitage, if I succeed—and I am certain to, I think, for I know that I have her love—you must perform the—the ceremony."

It was really odd how much Arnold stammered, and how wild his grammar became in the course of this sentence. Armitage said nothing, but laid a friendly hand on his shoulder.

"As for the rest of it, you can learn it from Paston. I can't talk about it now. It is now, at the last moment, that one feels one's utter unworthiness. You count humility a virtue— when a man is in my position," said Arnold, the smile breaking out on his face again, "he ought to be virtuous; for, upon my word, I never felt so humble in my life before."

"With the cheerful prospect of a reaction in the way of inordinate arrogance in a couple of days. Well, my friend, I won't chaff you—I must leave you here." They paused, and stood holding each other by the hand in a warm grip. "And do you know, in spite of what I said just now, I

can almost find it in my heart to envy you.
Good-bye."

They parted, and Arnold watched the other
turn down to visit a humble cottage where there
were two children down with fever.

"Well," he said, as he strolled homeward,
musing, "who knows? You too, one way or
another, will have your reward—something better
than a bishopric."

It is to be observed that Arnold's confidence
in the reception he would meet with at Burnport
was justified by the entire certainty that Ursula
loved him ; and that being so, he knew that whatever anxiety he might naturally feel, the issue
was really pretty secure. He had talked of the
matter to no one but Paston, and was relieved to
find that the astute doctor was so safe a confidant, though he had himself now been moved
to speak of it to Armitage.

While he was wending his way homeward, the
intellectual offspring of Confucius and all the
Ptolemies was holding high converse with Mrs.
Marchpane in the comfortable housekeeper's room
at Oakleigh.

"What I says, Mrs. Marchpane, is as sich
conduck is no-ways to be reck'ned on. 'Ere's
Mr. Arnold bin a gally-wantin' fust of all in
furrin parts for a year, an' then when he come
back, what does he do? Settle down quiet with

his pipe an' a missus? Nary a bit. Off he goes
a gally-wantin' again down to the sea, as Providence didn't mean us to go a riskin' our precious lives on, else fur why wur England made
into a island? an' when he's done a-tryin' to
drownd hisself, 'e can't come back 'ere quiet an'
respectable like, but takes his-self off to Lunnon,
an' spends his blessed time, for what I can see, a
meddlin' with other chaps as don't b'long to his
spear, nor didn't ought to. An' what's he got
fur it all? jest a bit of a tumble as knocked 'im
up a bit a year ago. Looks as if there couldn't
be a brighter side o' things nohow." Mr. Gibbins
rubbed his chin in deep disgust at this persistent
defiance of fortune.

"There now, Joshua, I never did see such a
cantankerous man as you are," said the housekeeper. "Why should he be hurting himself so?
You never seem to be content, I declare, unless
you hear that somebody's been breaking their
arms or legs, or something. Why, if you weren't
as pleased as pleased when old John's little girl
got scarlatina, and now you want the young
master to break his neck, I do believe."

"Well," responded the sage, "an' a good thing
it wur too as she did get it; them things is best
took young, an' so you ought to ha' knowed, mum.
An' that 'ere's jest what you women's always a
doin', a-twistin' round what a man says till 'e

don't know whether 'e's a standin' on 'is 'ead or
'is 'eels. I says, Mr. Arnold ha' bin a gally-
wantin', an' round comes you a sayin' as I wants
'im to break his neck! Men-folks is mostly fools,
mum; but there—they ain't a patch on women."

Now Mrs. Marchpane was no more inclined
than Mr. Gibbins himself to express approbation
of her master's wandering proclivities; but then
it was not at all her way to suffer anyone but
herself to comment on Arnold's failings. And
when Joshua added to this primary encroach-
ment on her own particular prerogative one of
those sweeping denunciations of the sex which
he generally kept compressed within him till he
was fortified in the security of his own den, it
was more than her equanimity could endure.

"My certies," she exclaimed, "to think o' you
talking like that! Why, Rhoda there"—the
housemaid entered at the moment—"has got as
much sense in her little finger as there is in all
your big body. Sakes alive! as if the master
mightn't go where he likes without your opinion.
And what would he want to be marrying for at
his years?" Mrs. Marchpane's round countenance positively glowed with indignation.

But the philosopher bore the attack as became
him, calmly.

"I ain't a-sayin' anything agin' partickler persons, mum: Rhoda, she's a gal as knows what

she's about when she's a mindin' of her own business, as she mostly hev the sense to do, an' I
don't say as she don't. But for gen'ral folly,
an' a-mixin' up o' things, an' a-tidyin' as is jest
makin' of a wuss mess nor before, an' for a
jumpin' at idees when they ain't got nothin' to
jump from, give me women."

Barbara could only fume. "Which I wonder
where the men 'ud be without us," put in Rhoda,
coming to her superior's assistance.

"Where 'ud the men be? if you'll go an' open
that 'ere big Bible o' Mrs. Marchpane's, an' search
the Scripturs, as the 'postle Paul says some-
wheres, round about them chapters at the beginnin', you'll see where we'd ha' bin, if it 'adn't
bin fur the con-trariness o' womankind, a-meddlin'
where they didn't ought to wi' their curosity,
a pokin' 'ere an' a pokin' there,—sittin' in Eden
we'd a' bin, 'stead o' eatin' by the sweat of
our brows. Mrs. Marchpane, mum, there's the
master's bell a ringin' for you."

And the triumphant Joshua retired with all
the honours to the privacy of his sanctum.

Ten minutes later, as Mrs. Marchpane came
out of Arnold's library, Paston walked into it,
with a flower in his button-hole, which he had
not been wearing when he left Oakleigh that
afternoon.

"Oh, Paston, Paston!" said Robur, turning

on him as the door closed; "oh, Machiavellian physician! How are the family at Beau Séjour? How is your young friend Frank? and—has Miss Dalton found anyone to marry her yet? And—where, my Benedick, where did that flower come from?"

"From the conservatory," replied the doctor with brazen countenance. "You see, my dear fellow, your fulcrum seemed to me to have answered the purpose so admirably that—well—I thought I might as well take a leaf out of your book. Pretty flower, isn't it?"

Joshua Gibbins, who was congratulating himself on an unwontedly brilliant victory over the housekeeper, was startled in the midst of his meditations by his door being suddenly thrown open, and the housekeeper herself appearing breathless in the opening. He was aghast at the intrusion—too much aghast to speak.

"Joshua," said Mrs. Marchpane before he had recovered, "Joshua, what d' you think? You're not to breathe a word of it to any living soul —but—he's going to bring back a—a missus. There, I'm an old fool"—the good soul's eyes were brimming over with joyful tears—"but— God bless 'em!" And she vanished.

Gibbins rose. The full import of Barbara's remarks was slowly becoming apparent to his

brain. He rubbed his. brow ; his eyes twinkled ;
he grinned ; suddenly the walls echoed one vast
"Ho ! ho !" Then Joshua raised his right hand
high in the air and brought it down on his thigh
with a sounding smack.

"Lor !" he said. "Blessed if 'ere don't seem
to be a brighter side o' things arter all !"

# CHAPTER XIV.

### JOANNA LOOKS OUT OF THE WINDOW.

" O fond anxiety of mortal men !
How vain and inconclusive arguments
Are those which make thee beat thy wings below !
For statutes one, and one for aphorisms
Was hunting : this the priesthood follow'd, that
By force or sophistry aspir'd to rule ;
To rob another, and another sought
By civil business wealth ; one moiling lay
Tangled in net of sensual delight,
And one to wistless indolence resign'd ;
What time from all these empty things escap'd,
With Beatrice, I thus gloriously
Was rais'd aloft, and made the guest of heav'n."

*Divina Commedia* (Cary's translation).

AUNT Joan looked out of the window.

It was a simple act, but her way of doing it made it expressive. She had caught the trick a year ago, almost immediately after a certain event which had nearly affected her own life and the lives of those dearest to her. Ursula used to wonder what it meant at first ; but gradually, as it grew into a habit, she ceased to notice, or at least to speculate about it. Once she might have thought that Joanna was expecting some thing—a letter, possibly—which never came; now she never thought about it, except as a harmless idiosyncrasy, having no significance to anyone, not even to the half-unconscious watcher herself.

Perhaps Ursula was more changed than Aunt Joan—changed, that is, not radically, but in the sense of being far more completely developed than she was a twelvemonth since. Outwardly things went on much the same at East Rise as they had done in previous years; Ursula had formed no new habits, though she did not disguise from herself that she was living a new life. Some casual mention of Arnold Robur would now and then escape Aunt Joan's lips, but not often. When she did speak of him, however, it was with perfect frankness, and the girl listened intently to such occasional news of him as there was to tell, saying little about it, but betraying no embarrassment when the topic was broached.

The remaining member of the family,—last, but not least,—Miss Hilda, was the only one who could boast that she had successfully resisted every subversive influence for a very long time back; in fact, her astounding immutability made farther demonstration that she was an immortal being almost superfluous. Nothing short of a universal cataclysm seemed ever likely to disturb the sanctified repose of the Mother Superior, nor was the blissful haven of her arm-chair to be submerged by any ordinary domestic storm. To put the matter as she herself once eloquently expressed it to her sadly recalcitrant sister :

"No one who believes in the special inter-position of Providence, Joanna, dearest, has any cause for unthankfulness, even when Earthquake, Famine, Pestilence, and Volcano are permitted to take their walks abroad."

On this particular February morning Miss Blunsden went forth armed in sweet trustfulness and thick furs to take an airing on the parade in her bath-chair. She was not accompanied by either of the other ladies, but her serene equa-bility was in no wise disturbed on that account. Sleep would doubtless console her for their ab-sence, she reflected, and an extra siesta thrown in before lunch do more to make her forget her cares than their somewhat unsympathetic com-pany. So without troubling them with an in-vitation to join her she departed, leaving Joanna sitting for her portrait to Ursula. The work was now nearly completed, and when the young artist laid down her implements, remarking that one more sitting would be all that was needed, her model graciously expressed a firm opinion that the likeness would after all turn out to be not unrecognisable.

It was after paying this compliment that Aunt Joan walked to the window and looked out.

Someone was coming up the hill. An exclamation rose to Joanna's lips, but she covered it with a cough, and went on watching the figure down below, while Ursula was occupied with her brushes. The individual in the road approached briskly, though he slackened his speed as he drew towards the house, and finally stopped before it in a rather hesitating manner.

"He's not going back now, surely," muttered Joanna to herself, keeping well beyond the range of the mysterious wayfarer's roving eyes.

Apparently he was unable to make up his mind to gain admittance just then, however. Swinging his stick meditatively in his hand, he advanced a little farther up the road, and disappeared down some rough steps which led to the garden in the glen below.

"Ursula, dear," said Aunt Joan, turning round quickly from the window, "go down to the drawing-room and clear your brains with a little music. I've got something I want to do now, and in half an hour we'll go out for a turn."

"Don't you be too long," said Ursula, as she prepared to acquiesce, "or we shan't have any time before lunch."

Joanna was suddenly in a great hurry for reasons of her own. She went to her room and slipped into walking habiliments ; then, as the sounds of the piano reached her, she stole downstairs, left a message with the servant that she would be back directly in case any one called, and with quiet promptitude let herself out of the house.

Her parting injunction to the maid was a source of much puzzlement to that invaluable domestic.

" Call ? Who's goin' to call this time o' day, I should like to know ? " quoth she, proceeding to polish her plate in the pantry.

The grim ogress had retired, leaving the castle undefended, and her captive princess all alone in it ; evidently, therefore, the prince's conduct would have been quite unjustifiable if he had not called, and been shown up into the bower where the princess was discoursing her sweet strains.

They sat down in the back drawing-room, where the piano was, did the prince and princess, he on an ottoman, she resuming her seat at the instrument ; and then they fell to talking.

" It is delightful," said he presently, " when friends can meet after a long interval and feel that each is the same to the other, however different the rest of the world may find them. People say, ' how changed you are ! ' but that is because they do not possess the key to one's heart. Friendship probes down at once into a man's inmost part, and discovers nothing there but what it knew and anticipated."

"Yes," returned she musingly; "friends can always tell how it will be with their friends; it seems to me that such men and women have the true spirit of prophecy."

He leaned his head on his hand and gazed at her:

"That is just what I think; second-sight can be no impossibility where 'Love is Law and Lord.'"

She started, trembling. Could he know what strange confirmation of their import his words conveyed?

He paused, but she did not open her lips, and he went on again, speaking very slowly:

"There is something I should have told you long ago, but could not find how I might do so before. Even now it is hard to say what I mean so that you may not misjudge me. Forgive me if the truth sounds hard when I tell it: believe that my part has been and is no less hard to play than yours."

She understood now. Silently she drew the ring from her finger, and laid it down by her on the piano.

He rose to take it, feeling the hand thrill that held it.

"This has been a symbol to you of much," he said; "it is in your power to say whether it shall ever mean more to you, or keep only the memory of what it has been to others before you. No one else has worn it since my mother laid it aside as the last relic of the love which she had known on earth, when she could have no farther use for any symbol. Then I missed it, and thought for a time that I should never be able to give it to the woman who could return my love. May that fear prove to have been vain! How it at last found its way to you is no matter, even if it were accurately known. What need to ask that question, when the gift that came to you by other hands was freely given by him who should have offered it? I own that the first sight of it upon your finger was so strange and inexplicable that at first I was carried out of myself, weakly drawn after some monstrous delusion. The past was all distorted when I looked back upon it: there was no solitary fact in my dealings with you or others about which I could feel any degree of sureness; nothing clearly cut or comprehensible enough to rid me of distrust and heal my folly. So things went on in aimless fashion, till I found one who taught me the doubt-dispelling power of love,—the love that I had tried in my feeble arrogance to forswear,— and then I easily understood my error.

U 2

"And now, Ursula, dear lady, let me know if you can accept this account of me, before I go on, and dare to ask more of you than forgiveness."

There were tears in her eyes as she fixed them with fond pride upon her knight, and a smile of praise and encouragement parted her lips as she made answer:

"Indeed, it does hurt me, as you say, to be deprived of associations such as have made that keepsake dear to me. But, after all, they were slight,—very slight,—even had they been true. The thought of them is soon gone, as all memory fades before the endless promise of the future. Oh, my dear, you are generous to take from me one little circumstance of sorrowful joy, putting in its place a vision of happiness whole and untainted. You no longer doubt your love, you tell me; but what if your doubts were right? I have never concealed myself from you, Arnold, and should not have put difficulties in your path of my own accord if it had been otherwise free. But are you sure you know how shallow, how ignorant, how narrow I really am? I am not afraid of debasing myself by saying so: better to acknowledge all this honestly than suffer you to be misled by any false pretence on my part. You have been open with me, and I am bound to be no less sincere with you. Perhaps I ought

to take the sternest view of my responsibility in
this, and refuse to tie you by anything more
binding than my dearest friendship. Surely men
and women may love each other without an ex-
clusive mutual engagement. You think too well
of me now, and would have me take advantage
of your infatuation."

She spoke with a concentrated animation that
he had never seen in her, or any other woman,
before. Her eyes sparkled now and again, and
there was a faint flush in her cheek; but she
remained in her former posture, bearing herself
with calm earnestness.

Arnold began to walk up and down, as was
his way when he had any knotty matter to
disentangle.

"Well, well; if to be as I am is to be in-
fatuated, there is only one being who can trans-
mute my passion into something more rational,
or work any other change in me that she will.
Has she faults? I suppose so, though they are
veiled to human eyes. No, Ursula," he came
and stood before her, "I will not let you answer
me like that. Marriage is not a question of
deserts on either side; fair maidens have never
yet held competitive examinations to test the
worth of the successful lover, and an infatuation
does not outlive such an absence as mine has

been. You might have thought good to refuse me utterly; then I should not have pressed you farther. But now, knowing as much of you as I can understand, I beseech you to let me learn more. Already I am wiser than I was; the love I bear you has made me more alive to all else in the world, I think; and that again— the comparing of you with every other object of desire—led me back by a new road to perceiving your excellence afresh. So far, dear girl, the lesson has been faithfully learned: beyond this point I cannot go alone; you must be with me, if I am to explore all that is still denied me."

"It is all so strange," said Ursula, pressing her hands over her eyes; "bear with me, I must realise it gradually."

Arnold gave her time. His heart beat fast with exulting gladness: she was his at last; no need to hurry now.

He sat down again, his head swimming with the sudden reaction of this long-continued strain upon his faculties, while his ears seemed stunned by the jubilant rhythm of some great hymn of praise. To him, too, sheer bewilderment was the first consequence of the overwhelming harvest of his hopes. There was nothing to be done but to begin reaping the fruits before him; but for a space his senses almost failed, appalled at the prodigious task. A moment since, as it were, he had been starving; and now he could not take and eat for very plenty.

Why should attainment of our ambitions be so often attended with pain, not only in the getting, but even when what we want is actually grasped? Men work, strive, push, pant, agonise for enjoyment which, when all has been done to win it, they cannot enjoy. Nor are the wisest and greatest any better off than the meanest in this respect. Alexander, and the most miserable slave in Alexander's dominions, were equally subject to the impartial administration of this law: both were doomed to dissatisfaction,—the one with his black bread and offal, the other with each fresh accession of territory that crowned his victories.

But the lovers, while they felt this, knew that to be dissatisfied is the greatest prerogative that man or woman can possess. The true ideal is too far beyond for any one of the successive stages in the approach to it to be regarded as final, when once such temporary shelter has been gained. They had passed but the foot-hills, and began to see for the first time a distinct outline of heights yet to be traversed, whose top reached unto heaven.

"Are there many other people in the world for whom you care?" asked Ursula abruptly.

"Yes, to be sure; there's Aunt Joan, and all my old friends at home, to say nothing of Paston, and Armitage, and the Daltons—some of them; besides a few school and college associates. Then there are a number of my Whitechapel neighbours of whom I have managed to get very fond somehow during the past year, and some of them have been down to see me for a few days at Oakleigh. Oh, my visiting list is quite a goodly roll, Ursula, and I can assure you that I really like everyone whose name is on it, more or less."

"It sounds like a reproach," returned she a little mournfully; "here have I been living on for years and years, never getting to know anyone, scarcely, out of our own small circle here. How shall I make others take to me as they do to you? My sympathies may be permanently stunted, and by my own fault too. I don't see how anyone is ever likely to feel the least concern about me, except you and dear Aunt Joan. I don't deserve to be loved at all,—a heartless, self-willed creature, like Beatrix in the play."

Arnold laughed.

"A woman's view of that gracious, generous lady! But give your sympathies the chance, love. Trust me, air and exercise is all they want."

Gaiety is catching, and Ursula's face grew mirthful.

"Well, you must give me a trial," she said with the old delicious ripple in her voice. "What do you say to asking Aunt Joan to bring me to Oakleigh for a month on approval? Not that I anticipate not liking the place, but just to see how the place likes me. Do you think you can give us board and lodging on those terms?"

"Speaking for Mrs. Marchpane and myself, I think I may say that the arrangement is as good as made," was Arnold's reply. "But aren't you more like Miranda than Beatrix to let your first male friend woo so successfully?"

"A very naughty as well as clumsy attempt at humour, sir!" and Ursula tried to look severe. "Such wickedness must be made an immediate example of, or there is no knowing to what crimes it may lead. Perhaps you are not aware that a most powerful rival has been in the field before you, and one who, I am sure, whatever else his faults may be, would never have made me the victim of a classical allusion."

Arnold's look of wonderment was changed to an amused grimace when he heard the conclusion of this scathing rebuke.

"Poor Frank," said he, smiling; "I suppose you gave him a dreadful lecture; I hope you had as much pity on him as you have showed to me."

"Not quite as much," replied Ursula mischievously; "I keep my pity for those who need it most, you see. Frank Dalton's was quite a transient attack, and was not attended with deeply injurious results. In fact, I saw a good deal more of him after the outbreak than before. He used to come to me for advice, so I suppose my behaviour on that momentous occasion must have inspired him with awe and admiration of my brilliant sagacity. We talked his matters over ever so many times; he only wanted to get away from his mother to become a very good sort of boy, and I believe we really did each other some good."

"Yes," remarked her lover; "I happen to know that was the case on one side, at any rate. You didn't miss the opportunity of extending your sympathies then, Ursula. Frank Dalton owes his start in life to you almost as much as I do."

They were close together, and he took her hand.

"Arnold," she said, "do not let us wrap ourselves up alone in our love, dear. Love must die, if it cannot have the whole world free for it to settle everywhere, and make honey in as it will and of what it will. A single tiny cottage garden—or even the Oakleigh one—is no sufficient scope for its untiring work. You have been thoughtful for others without me, and I do not want you to be less unselfish when I come to you. I must help you all I can to keep up your friends—my friends,—and even add to their number."

"Yes, yes, my darling; oh, Ursula, how good you are, how blest I am!"

Another long eloquent silence followed. Sweet as was the present, they were each thinking rather of the past which led them to it, of the future to which it led. Here at this supreme crisis of their lives they saw, with that magical insight, which for the moment possessed their souls, how every fact and circumstance had traced its delicate converging line to this point of time, and how a myriad more were to diverge again from it, presaging unutterable things.

*    *    *    *    *

The hall-door below was opened, and there were sounds of voices, one of which was raised to a rather unusual pitch, but not apparently for purposes of altercation.

Aunt Joan was talking to her sister; they had reached the foot of the stairs, and now seemed to be ascending.

Then the prince took the ring, and placed it again upon the princess's yielding finger, just where it had been before. Having done this, he bent down tenderly over her, and kissed her between the eyes; and they two were happy.

## THE END.

R. Clay and Sons, Bungay, Suffolk.

www.ingramcontent.com/pod-product-compliance
Lightning Source LLC
Chambersburg PA
CBHW060555030726
47498CB00005B/1395